I0556229

OUT OF THE MIST

OUT OF THE MIST

22 Atlantic Canadian Ghost Stories

Evergreen Writers Group

Out of the Mist
22 Atlantic Canadian Ghost Stories

Copyright ©2014
Stone Cellar Publications
Halifax/Dartmouth, Nova Scotia

ISBN-13: 978-0993833809
ISBN-10: 0993833802
June 2014

Edited by Pamela Gifford

Cover photo: Camp Hill Cemetery, Halifax, NS,
by Phil Yeats

All stories contained in this volume have been published with permission of the authors.

No portion of this publication may be reproduced, stored in any electronic system, or transmitted in any form or by any means, electronic, mechanical, photocopy, recording, or otherwise without written permission from the authors.

Although some of the stories may be inspired by real events and may name a few historical people and facts, the majority of these stories are works of fiction. In most cases, names, characters, businesses, places, events, and incidents are either products of the authors' imaginations or used in a fictitious manner. Except for several named historical characters long deceased, any resemblance to actual persons, living or dead, is purely coincidental.

***

Facebook page:
https://www.facebook.com/EvergreenWritersGhostAnthology

Preface

Inspired by the tales of renowned folklorist Helen Creighton, a group of writers decided to try their hand at an anthology of ghost stories. Perhaps it's the photograph of Ms. Creighton in her writing room, or the chill air in the old stone cellar where we meet, but we felt her presence hovering over us. We decided to call our group Evergreen Writers, in honor of the house and its famous inhabitant.

Written over a period of 18 months, these stories point to other worlds, other times that lie just beyond the thin veil that separates us. Many take place in a house with a long history, whose descendants still speak of the strange events that happened there. Some stories are inspired by real events; others are entirely the author's imagination.

Whether you're a visitor to Atlantic Canada or have always lived here, these stories will entertain you, mystify you and perhaps give you the shivers.

The Evergreen Writers

Appreciation

The Evergreen Writers Group thanks our editor, Pamela Gifford, for her attentive care and suggestions.

We also thank the Dartmouth Heritage Museum's Evergreen House and the Alderney Gate Branch, Halifax Regional Library, in whose pleasant meeting rooms we shared stories and made the many decisions leading to the publication of this volume. The resources provided by libraries and museums are deeply appreciated by writers everywhere.

Table of Contents

The Voices of Dawnbrook
Manon Boudreau

The sweet scent of autumn leaves lies thick in the air, and I tug my jacket higher around my neck to ward off a chill. I sip on my coffee and stare at the property in front of me. Nearby on the mansion's metal fence is perched a crow, its caws a raw greeting.

What started as a research assignment for the *Historical Journal of the Maritimes* quickly grew into an obsession. There was something strange about the town of Chatham, New Brunswick. The census for the years 1880 to 1890 showed a child mortality rate 18 percent higher than any of the other surrounding communities.

Some families lost more than one child, but only one family lost all of them. Dawnbrook Mansion, silent and empty now, was the home of Anne and Wilfred Fisher and their four children from 1886 to 1895. In the space of 18 short months, all four children died.

I'm fevered at the thought of what awaits me inside the mansion. Desolate and grim, sitting in a field blighted by discarded beer cans and fast food wrappers, the building is a far cry from its former self. You can see a glimpse of its dusty beauty when you look closely at the frame, the bones of the building. Overgrown weeds and garbage hide what was once a stunning sight. But more than that, the history inside the house is like no other I've found.

The head of the *Maritime Historical Society*, Edith Brylar, waves to me from the front porch. She is an elderly plump woman with big-frame eye glasses and a cap of curly grey hair.

She fumbles with the key to the front door.

"Hello, Catherine," she says. "You found the place OK?"

The door groans in protest as she pushes it open. I hurry towards the entrance as a nervous giggle escapes my lips, and I cough to cover it.

"Yes, no problems on the road," I tell her. "Thank you so much for meeting me."

She enters the mansion and motions for me to follow. Festooned with cobwebs and dust, the entrance is still an awe-inspiring sight. I can make out the spiral staircase and the remnants of a gilt picture hung over a broken-down pianoforte. Paired with the tall ceiling and the chandeliers, it suggests a former elegance.

I carefully take a few steps in, cautious not to disturb even the dust. Edith leads me to what would have been the sitting room.

"Throughout the home, you'll find all the original woodwork still intact," she tells me. "After the untimely passing of her first born, Mrs. Fisher fell into a deep depression. Her journals detailed the dark place she fell into after her son was found dead. Mr. Fisher had the wood imported from the Far East and as a show of love, built this room for Mrs. Fisher. It certainly is grand; however, it is only a mere attempt at redemption, if you ask me," she adds, a note of bitterness in her tone.

Built into each wall are library shelves, now naked of books. I can imagine Mrs. Fisher sitting at a carved mahogany desk, reading from one of her books, or perhaps catching up on correspondence. She would have received guests here, and discussed current affairs.

"Redemption for what?" I ask her.

"He was never arrested, but the rumours were that he was involved in the death of the children." She gestures towards the extensive shelves, effectively changing the subject. "Quite a sight isn't it?"

My eyes light on a frame leaning against the bottom of the far wall. It is a painting. My body moves of its own accord towards it. It's a painting of the mansion during its glory days. I've seen many photographs and they gave me much insight as to the state of the property in the 1890s, but this painting is something else.

The artist captured such depth and raw energy. The landscape depicts the fountain and its surrounding bushes, trees and flowers, but it is drenched in sorrow. I gently rub the layer of dust off the lower right corner of the frame, and find the artist's name and the date.

Anne Fisher painted this during the month of June 1894, one month after Mary, the last of her four children, died. As beautiful as the property was, it must have been purgatory for her. The sheer madness of losing a child overwhelms me. It's unnatural. Still holding the painting, I turn to Edith.

"How did little Mary die?" I ask her. She lifts an eyebrow in surprise.

"A broken neck. She fell from the large oak tree in the back of the property. No one saw how it happened. Mr. Fisher was the one who found her, just like he found the other three."

An uncontrollable shiver runs through my body.

"If you don't have any questions, let's move on. The side veranda is just this way," says Edith. "It's in need of repair, but the view is lovely this time of year."

A noise overhead startles me. It sounds like an object is being dragged across the floor above me. I learned some time ago not to be unnerved by the creaking of old homes and buildings, so I brush off the noise. Old houses sag and shift on their foundations over time. The noises are part of that process.

Edith leads me to the left side of the mansion. The veranda has suffered more damage than the other parts of the building. Being exposed to the elements for years has rotted the wood. It is partly enclosed, and was surely stunning at one point. But now it hardly seems to fit with the rest of the mansion. Edith cautions me not to go farther.

"If you'll notice the chairs at the far end corner," she adds. "Mr. Fisher carved them himself. His tools are still in the outbuilding."

One of the chairs is smaller than the others. It's the size of a toy.

"Did Mr. Fisher make toys for his children as well?" I ask Edith.

"We believe he did. We found wooden dolls' furniture and doll-size bassinets in a playhouse outside, and a doll house in the girls' room," she answers.

The dragging sound catches my attention again. "What do you think that noise is?"

"Just the sounds of an old house," she mutters. "The mansion needs repair. It will be added to the *Registry of Historic Buildings* shortly. Restoration can commence then," she says, and stalks off. "Are you ready to see the ballroom?"

I cast a look outside before turning. The temperature has dropped, and the sky is filled with clouds pregnant with rain. I snap pictures of the veranda from every angle, and also take a few of the small chair.

"Sure," I reply and chase after her.

"All the bedrooms are upstairs. We can get to those afterwards," Edith tells me. "I'm sure you have some interest in the nursery and children's rooms.

"How did Mr. Fisher die?" I ask.

Edith pauses in the hall, and turns towards me. "He jumped from the second floor of this house. One of the maids, Evelyn Brylar, found him the next morning. She was his mistress."

I scribble some notes as she shares this information. On our way to the ballroom, we pass the great hall. It's large enough to have served as an entertainment space. I snap pictures of the elaborate mouldings and frames.

"The Fishers entertained here frequently," mentions Edith.

I pause to look at a collection of dolls lined up on a settee. I feel distressed at the sight of all these toys. How lamentable it must have been after the death of their owners.

"How did the first three children pass away?" I ask.

We enter the ballroom. I raise my camera to begin snapping photos. I feel like I'm eight again, watching Beauty and the Beast dance on the screen. Edith walks past me, and lays a hand on the mantel.

"The firstborn was a boy, Wilfred, named after his father," she begins.

She runs her finger through the dust, then blows on it.

"Mr. Fisher kept journals. Wilfred, Jr., seemed exceptional, if perhaps a bit spoiled. His mother doted on him," she says. "She waited eight years to finally have a child. Who could blame her? In his journal, Mr. Fisher described feeling jealous of his son. He began his affair with Evelyn Brylar shortly after the boy turned a year old."

The dragging noise upstairs starts again. "How old was Wilfred Junior when he died?" I ask, and stare at the ceiling in puzzlement.

She walks towards a painting lying on the floor. She picks it up and leans it against the wall.

"He was six. He was playing with the family dog by the brook, just about a hundred yards from the house. According to the reports, Mr. Fisher told the authorities he heard his son scream and he ran towards his voice. At the brook, he found the child lying face down in the shallow water. It is said the water barely reached his knees."

I inhale deeply and tighten my scarf. It's cold. The dragging noise starts again.

"Did anyone see how it happened?"

"No. Mr. Fisher was the only one who saw anything," she replies. "Let's go upstairs. I'll show you the nursery and bedrooms. Most of the children's furniture is still intact."

I put my camera back in my shoulder bag, and write down some more information. "That should be interesting. Thank you."

Each step creaks under our weight. Everything upstairs is covered in a layer of dust. We walk into an open area furnished with four chairs decoratively placed around a wooden centre table. Short hallways lead into the main bedroom, two guest rooms, two children's bedrooms, and the nursery.

"What happened to the girls?" I ask Edith.

She opens a wooden chest, and coughs as a result of escaping dust.

"The second born, Elizabeth, died six months after her brother. She was five years old. Elizabeth and Leslie shared this room here, the one to the left."

I follow her into the girls' room as she continues. "Mr. Fisher built a playhouse for the children behind the mansion. One of the maids saw Elizabeth running towards it."

I take my camera out again, and capture the girls' room. It is painted and decorated completely in white.

"The maid said she seemed fine at the time," she adds.

I snap pictures of the toys and furniture. The doll house Mr. Fisher built sits by the windows. It's a masterpiece of intricately detailed rooms.

"What happened to her?"

"Mr. Fisher found her dead at the bottom of the playhouse, with Belladonna berries in her hand. The doctors said she'd eaten a fatal amount."

"That's terrible!"

"It is, but you see the berries she ate, they didn't grow on the property. Someone must have given them to her. During the week of Elizabeth's death, two other girls in the area about the same age died of poisoning."

There's a painting of the girls sitting on a dresser. They look to be about three and four.

"Elizabeth and Leslie were 11 months apart. It is said they were more like twins than sisters," says Edith.

They look strikingly alike. They both have shoulder-length blonde hair and dimples.

"They do look more like twins than sisters. Leslie must have been devastated after her sister's death."

"She was. She got sick shortly after. She spent the next two weeks in bed."

"Is that how she died? Was it from the sickness?"

The town suffered an epidemic of influenza during the mid-1890s. It would have been a likely cause of death.

"No, she died in the barn, where the family kept horses. She enjoyed spending time with them and feeding them apples. The authorities couldn't understand how, but the horses got out and she was trampled," she says. "After the first two children died, they watched the family more closely. But sadly, there were also many children's deaths in the town. They didn't have any official suspects."

The feeling of sadness again overwhelms me.

"Let me show you the nursery," she says.

The same dragging sound is back, except this time it is close. My curiosity gets the best of me this time. The noise is coming from the sitting area. I quickly head out of the girls' room and into the hall. It's dark, and at the end of the short hallway from the girls' room, I run into an object. I hit the ground with a thump, knocking the wind out of me. Edith runs over.

"Are you okay?" she asks, a twinge of panic in her voice.

"I ran into this chair." I mumble the obvious.

She turns around, and picks up a wooden chair and stands it back upright. I recognize it from the sitting area.

"This wasn't here when we went in the girls' room," she says.

"I didn't see a chair either," I say, rubbing my left knee.

I notice dragging marks on the floor. They lead to where the chair was. "Look, Edith. The chair was dragged here. Look! Look at the tracks!"

Surprised, she studies the chair more closely. "It must be teenagers playing tricks. We get a call or two every month of kids hanging around here," she quickly rationalizes. "Are you okay to walk, or should I call for help?"

Short of a few bruises, I'm okay. My ego seems to have taken the worst of it. I take the chair and follow the dragging marks in the dust. They bring me back to the seating area. I put it back in its place with more force than necessary.

"You mentioned we should see the nursery next," I tell Edith, redirecting us to the task at hand.

"It's on the other side of the sitting area, down another short hallway," she replies.

I follow Edith into the hall, and cast a spiteful look at the chair. Perplexed, I search the ground for an additional pair of footprints but find only mine and Edith's.

The nursery looks different from the other rooms. It is soft, cheerful and unassuming. It doesn't have the same air of formality. It's lovely.

"This is where Mrs. Fisher hanged herself," announces Edith, pointing at the doorway. "It happened six weeks after she lost her fourth child."

I shudder visibly. "Who found her?"

"One of the maids, Evelyn. The same one who found Mr. Fisher." She pauses. "Evelyn Brylar was my great-grandmother." Her tone is guarded, and piques my curiosity.

"Did Evelyn pass on any accounts of the incidents?"

"Some. She kept correspondence of that time. Several of the richer families in Chatham were dealing with the death of one or more of their own children," she says. "However, she didn't write about her own suspicions, but mostly about her own children, whom she missed terribly. She thought the Fishers were cruel to send her children away."

How lamentable is this house's history.

"She was the maid who had an affair with Mr. Fisher, wasn't she?" I ask.

"Yes, she was 22 when the affair began. She bore three of his children, who were sent away to be cared for by relatives of hers. It would have been unseemly to have the children in the same house as Mrs. Fisher."

I feel disgusted. What a bleak story this research assignment was turning out to be.

"How long after Leslie did the fourth child, Mary, die?"

"Only three weeks. During that month, five of the town's children died. All of them were from affluent families. They all died from what appeared to be accidents. No witnesses were ever found, and no one was charged. Mr. Fisher was the only suspect they had. When he was interviewed, there were some inconsistencies in his statement. His whereabouts couldn't be explained during the death of some of the children.

"Every child who died also had some connections to the Fishers. Some of the families were friends and some were associates of Mr. Fisher. They were all from the richer families. Though many believed him guilty, no tangible evidence was ever found."

I visibly jump when I hear the dragging sound start again.

"They're back!" I whisper to Edith.

This time, I mean to see what is going on. I quietly tiptoe out of the nursery, and into the small hall. At the end of the hall, the same chair is there.

"Those darn kids!" I mutter.

Dragging marks are visible leading to the chair. I look for footprints, or a sign that would lead me to the culprits, but see nothing.

"Let's leave the chair there, and move on to the main bedroom," says Edith. "If we don't play their game, they will get bored and move along."

Fine plan! In the lavishly decorated bedroom, I snap dozens of pictures, and secretly wish my bedroom looked like this.

"Is this where Mr. Fisher committed suicide?" I ask Edith.

"Yes, from this window over here," she says, as she leads me to the far wall. "When questioned, Evelyn stated that Mr. Fisher was drinking wine all evening, becoming increasingly loud and destructive, breaking pieces of art and furniture. Three empty wine bottles were found in this room the next morning. He was an odd sort of fellow, some said. Many were convinced Chatham had a serial killer, and that it was Mr. Fisher."

An entire family dead within 18 months.... I peer down from the window. His body would have landed in the middle of the driveway, for all to see.

"Were the authorities sure it was suicide? I mean, he wasn't pushed?"

"After the death of the children and his wife, Mr. Fisher retreated into isolation. He spent days in the dark, writing and muttering to himself. He left a letter on his bed before jumping. I have copies if you wish to see them. After his death, no other children died. Many thought that was proof enough of his guilt."

The dragging sound is back, but this time we ignore it. It stops close by, probably at the entrance of the short hall to the master bedroom. I snap a few pictures of the window and of the view. It is quiet in the hall.

"What about Mrs. Fisher? How did she die?"

"It happened right over there," she says as she points at the entrance to the nursery. "She hanged herself in the doorway. She jumped off a chair."

I feel a warm and tingly feeling throughout my body. I'm about to reply when I hear a sudden bang, as if something fell. We leave the master bedroom, to find the chair lying on its side at the entrance to the short hall.

"Which chair did Mrs. Fisher use?" I ask.

Edith stares at the fallen chair, and colour drains from her face. "I... I believe it was that one," she says, her voice trembling. "The chair... was lying on its side. Evelyn Brylar found her as well. She described it in a letter to her sister. The chair was on the floor, just like it is now."

My mind races for a rational explanation.

"It must be a coincidence," I assure her. "There are only three other chairs to choose from, after all."

I can see Edith is struggling to explain the incident. She clears her throat and regains some of her composure.

"Would you like to see the outer buildings? There is also the old oak tree at the back of the property."

"I think I've seen everything I needed, Edith. Thank you for the offer, but my paper will focus mainly on the inside of the mansion," I say, deliberately ignoring the chair.

We part ways at the entrance. I glance one last time at the stunning, intriguing mansion, and thank Edith profusely.

"You'll find copies of the suicide letters and some news clippings from the time in here," she states, handing me a thick envelope. "I'm sure they will be of interest to you."

Outside, it is raining heavily. I tug my jacket higher to cover my head, and run to my yellow Volkswagen Beetle, clutching my bag stuffed with the documents Edith gave me close, hoping to keep them dry.

At home, I'm alone in my house, and all is quiet. I settle at my writing desk with a cup of peppermint tea. I sip the warm liquid, as I read the first letter. A lone tear slides down my cheek and lands on the page.

Mrs. Fisher's letter speaks of a broken heart and a desire to be with her children. Nothing in this life seemed worth living without her babies. She was prepared to go and hoped that she would be reunited with her four children.

Mr. Fisher's letter was different. He too suffered terribly from the death of his children, but what pushed him over the edge was his wife's suicide. I put the letters down, feeling a sense of dread and fear grow in my belly.

Sweet innocent voices beckon me to turn my computer on. *It's time, Catherine. It's time to write.*

I feel the usual tickle of excitement when I start writing, but it is tainted with fear. I open a new document and write *The truth of Dawnbrook Mansion* as a title. I want to erase the first three words of the title, but my fingers won't cooperate. I wince in pain as I force my hands to move away from the keyboard.

Write, Catherine! You need to know what happened! the voices urge.

I try in vain to take my hands away from the keyboard. Strong, invisible forces keep them firmly in place. I am overcome with emotion and begin to weep.

Write, Catherine. The voices are more forceful this time.

"No, please stop. Please," I say between sobs.

The voices scream this time. *Write! Someone needs to know what happened to us.*

Tears sting my eyes. I keep fighting. I want to stop writing, but can't. Pain shoots up my fingers and creeps to my wrists. Tears trail down my face.

"What's happening?" I cry. "Please stop."

You need to write, Catherine. You need to write the truth.

Sweat beads on my forehead and neck. My fingers fly across the keyboard.

That's it, Catherine. The voice has calmed and now encourages me.

Crying, I continue writing. The words on the page are not mine.

Stop, Catherine, it says, at last.

Alarmed, I looked at the words on the screen. I feel a pounding rhythm in my head. I look aghast at the words I wrote, the words I was made to write.

Evelyn did it. Evelyn did it.

~~~***~~~

Avast There! Belay That!

Maida Follini

Captain Archie Edwards was a choleric man, a short, but muscular seaman with a red face and a short red beard. Navigating his three-masted schooner along the coast of Nova Scotia to ports in New England or sometimes as far as the Caribbean, he made a good living in the early 1900s, the final days of commercial sail. Enough to build an impressive Captain's Mansion at Edwards' Neck, the spit of land north of Shag Harbour, where his childhood had been spent in his parents' falling-down shack.

Some want to get away from an impoverished childhood. Arch wanted to conquer it. Starting in his teens as a hand on fishing sloops, he became mate on a coastal trader, and then earned his master's papers, studying navigation at night. Captaining other owner's vessels, he finally saved enough to buy a schooner of his own.

As a coming man, he courted one of Shag Harbour's belles, Amelia Comstock, daughter of Judge Comstock, and carried her off under the noses of several Halifax-educated lawyers and businessmen. Archie had ambition. He had his mansion built during his and Amelia's long engagement, and handed her over the threshold on his wedding day.

At sea, he ran a tight ship, always Master, driving his crew to his own demanding standards. Some say he never slept. At least he made sure his men never slept on their watch. Berating them, harassing them, blistering them with insults when a mistake was made, he had the reputation of a hard man, with a temper, not one to be crossed.

He was not one to show softness. Amelia and his mascots were the only ones he was close to. He always had a mascot. At first it was an affectionate Jack Russell terrier that traveled on his schooner with him. On land, for many years he had an old Canadian gander, a large grey-backed bird with a honking bill that would follow him down the street. Ludicrous though it was, no one laughed at Captain Archie. After the gander passed away (some said from overeating, as the Captain was generous with his mascots), Archie adopted an orphaned raven, which would perch on his shoulder like an evil genius. It flew around his head while he did the garden chores, and learned to talk in Captain Archie's hoarse voice: *"Avast, there!" "Straighten up!" "Blast your eyes!" "Belay that!"*

As for his wife, he might be heard shouting at everyone else, including his three daughters and young son, but he never raised his voice to Amelia. Formal politeness covered whatever deep emotions—whether love or anger—that lay between them. It is said that when she encountered his first bout of temper not long after they were married, she met it with calm disgust, and went on a very long visit to her father's home. He never showed his temper towards her again. She was a reserved, some said cold, woman used to leading town society, and not afraid to speak up, even to her father, the judge. She must have let Archie know she could do very well without him, because he had to come supplicating her to return to their house on Edwards' Neck.

Something fiery must have held them together. She never separated from him again, and they became parents of three daughters, and finally after a gap of years, they were blessed with a long-awaited son, Archie Edwards, Junior.

As a boy, Junior Edwards saw his father perhaps two months out of the year, as the Captain was away on voyages lasting three, four, or six months during the peak time of his trading life. Junior was soon nick-named "June", much to his father's disgust. He grew into a tall, gangly boy, all legs and arms, with a knack for falling out of trees, getting stung by wasps, and a genius for getting into awkward situations. His mother's darling, being her only boy, he was molly-coddled while his father was away, and bullied when his father was home. June rarely came up to his father's demanding expectations.

Handing a can of paint up to his father, who was painting the house, June managed to tip the paint can all over himself. "Clumsy idiot!" his father shouted, while his mother wrapped him in towels and took him inside for a bath. June couldn't seem to keep out of trouble. When a baseball went through a neighbour's window, the other boys managed to slip away through a hedge, and June was caught. On Hallowe'en, when he and his buddies removed a gate from the town hall fence, it was June whom a policeman collared while the other boys crouched out of sight in a ditch.

June was a cheerful chap, though, trying his best, and in spite of the constant criticism, he admired his father, and wanted to please him. When he was 14, he was thrilled when Captain Archie decided to take him on a three-month trading voyage on the schooner. Two weeks later, June returned on the train from Boston. He had been sea-sick, not just the usual couple of hours, or even a day, but the whole two weeks, alternately hanging over the rail, or bundled into his berth. On arriving back in Shag Harbour, June was not so much cast down as relieved to be in his own comforting home locale.

While his father was away, June faithfully looked after Captain Archie's mascot, the black raven that lived in the trees nearby and flew down to the kitchen door each morning for hand-outs. June would still be startled by its voice. *"Straighten Up!"* the raven would cry, and June's spine would stiffen as if his father were after him, even though the Captain was away. To June, constant harassment and criticism was normal, and he did not expect anything different.

As the twenties turned to the thirties, the coastal trade diminished. Captain Arch and Amelia saw their three daughters get married and leave home. The schooner remained tied at the wharf.

One day Captain Archie dropped down dead on the way home from an evening with his friends at the local saloon. Amelia placed a glowing obituary in the local paper, extolling her husband's virtues: his faithfulness, industry, and loving kindness. (His old crew members scarcely recognized him from the account.) Two years later, Amelia herself passed away with her usual calm dignity, in her own bed after a brief (undisclosed) illness. She left June, now age 27, to inherit the Edwards Mansion, and his share of funds in the bank.

June, in spite of his father's poor opinion of his capabilities, had started a successful business as a handy man, fixer, and doer of odd jobs for the community. His cheerfulness and willingness made him first choice when anyone had a fence to repair, a porch to paint, or a garden to dig.

That he also had money in the bank was well-known in the community, and in particular to Miss Darlene Sewall, who, in her early thirties lived with her mother in half a house, and was anxious to improve her situation. From helping her dig her garden, to accepting a cup of tea in her house, the acquaintance progressed to movie dates, and after several months, Darlene was being shown over the Mansion House at Edwards' Neck. Following the tour, Darlene lounged in a chair at the back porch, admiring the ocean view. She was smiling, and hopefully expecting a proposal of marriage. As a matter of fact, June sensed what was expected of him, and he usually tried to do what was expected. He didn't actually kneel down, but he was leaning towards Darlene, when a hoarse voice rasped, *"Avast there! Straighten Up!"* Automatically, June straightened his spine, looking round for his father.

"Nasty bird! Get away!" cried Darlene, flapping her hand at the raven.

June laughed. "No, it's just old Blacky," he explained. "He wants his hand-out." Humming a cheerful tune, June went into the kitchen, and came back with assorted dish scrapings. The bread crumbs, apple parings, and bits of bacon and egg left over from breakfast did not add a romantic atmosphere as he laid it out on a newspaper on the porch. The moment was gone.

That night, June ruminated as he lay in bed, watching through the window as the moon rose. His father, he knew, wouldn't have approved of Darlene. And he agreed with his father. Darlene had been a little too interested in the spacious house, the furniture, and particularly the silverware from his late mother's collection. The raven (or his father?) had helped him make a great escape.

The raven continued receiving hand-outs, sharing them with its mate and family which nested in the nearby spruce tree year after year. June's habit of helping people led him into a fellowship with an old school classmate, Jerry Neal, who was now a real estate man. Jerry took to coming over in the evening, and passing comments about how the town was growing. Jerry was connected to a man who wished to establish a hotel in Shag Harbour.

"You could go in with us, June," suggested Jerry. "You have an excellent site here, right on the water. My partner has experience in the hospitality trade. And I have some savings to invest." June was by nature agreeable to suggestions from his friends. A few evenings later, Jerry appeared with his partner, Melvin. Out on the back porch they all admired the view.

"You have a gold mine here." Melvin waved his hand at the harbour. "You could have a marina here on the shore. Add a motel wing to the Mansion. You have a gold mine."

June felt vaguely uncomfortable, rushed, some unpleasant feelings in his stomach. What would his mother have said? Or even more important, his father?

"Avast, there!" A flutter of black wings, a squawking bill. *"Blast your eyes!"* The bird seemed to be swearing at Melvin. *"Belay that!"* The yellow eyes glowered.

Dizziness took hold of June. His father had spoken. He was certain of that. Even the look in the raven's eyes had his father's glare. "No," he shook his head at his good buddy, Jerry. "I can't change the home my father built. It would be disrespectful."

He didn't even listen as they tried to persuade him. Disappointed and somewhat angry, the partners went away, Melvin shaking his head and saying, "You have a gold mine there."

At 35, June still lived in the Edwards Mansion, alone. People in town discussed his case.

"Everything to offer—house, income and money in the bank—and he's still alone!"

"Too much the mother's boy," said one.

"Too much Captain Edwards' bullying," said another.

"You get peculiar after living alone," said a third.

"He'll never marry, now."

But they were wrong.

One day, June found a young woman at the station struggling with her suitcase. He gave her a lift to the local restaurant, where she had come to take a job as cook. But when they arrived the proprietor came out of the kitchen, looking discomfited.

"Sorry, the position's been filled," he told the young woman. He shrugged. "My sister-in-law, she decided to take the job. You know how it is," he said, darting an unhappy glance at the partly open kitchen door.

"I'll have to go back to Halifax." Disappointed, the woman picked up her suitcase and turned away.

"Wait!" June said. "I need a cook. Come along with me."

After Sabrina moved in, June had the best meals he had eaten since his mother died.

The raven had the best hand-outs it had ever had, and never even had to squawk to ask for them. Sabrina kept its plate full and ready for it.

In three months, June and Sabrina were married. Before he was 45 years old, June was the father of Archie Edwards III, Amelia, and Little 'Rina, who cheerfully chased each other around the yard, fell out of trees, and broke windows playing ball. The raven family still nested in the spruce tree nearby, raising nestlings, and the calls would go back and forth: "Avast there!" June and Sabrina would call, and the ravens would cry back, *"Belay that!"* and *"Straighten Up! Blast your eyes!"*

~~~***~~~

Gran-gran's Ghost
Maida Follini

"Will Gran-gran stay in the box?" Evelyn whispered to Margaret, as they walked behind their mothers away from the flower-heaped coffin. Uncles, aunts, cousins had come up to the coffin after the funeral, stood with bowed heads, prayed, touched the sleek metal box, or taken a flower as a token from the array.

"Of course. She's dead!" Margaret replied. Margaret was seven while her cousin Evelyn was only five, and didn't know anything.

Once Margaret had seen a dead bird on the front walk and went to pick it up, but Dad had quickly scooped it up and thrown it in the compost bin, shutting the lid. "It will fall into a dust," Mother had consoled Margaret. "It will just become part of the compost, and then it will mix with the garden earth and help the plants grow."

That was what death was…at least…Margaret had once put her cat in a shoebox and covered it with the lid. Soon there had been a scrabbling noise, the lid bumped up, and an angry paw reached out. Seconds later, the whole cat emerged with an indignant scream and ran off. Could a dead person get out of a box? One that was shiny, metal, and fastened down tight? What if Gran-gran came alive in the box? Could she breathe? Wouldn't she be angry that the family had shut her in a box?

"I'm leaving Margaret and Evelyn here at the house," Mother told one of the aunts. "Young children shouldn't come to a burial. There'll be so many of us there, anyway." She looked around at Gran-gran's children—all grown up now. "We thought Margaret and Evelyn should be at the funeral so they could say good-bye to their grandmother, but that's enough. Can't expect them to be quiet and behave for too long."

Gran-gran's home seemed empty after the influx of relatives this morning. Mrs. Hemphill, Gran-gran's helper, was in the living room, placing flowers from mourners in vases. "I'll look after the little girls," she told Mother, taking them into the kitchen. She gave them some hot cocoa, and had them sit at the kitchen table where they wouldn't see the casket as it was carried out of the house and slid in the back of the hearse. Their mothers, fathers, uncles, aunts and older cousins got into their cars. Each vehicle sported a purple funeral flag. Within minutes the long procession disappeared from sight.

Margaret held her cup up high to look at the design, a picture of a flower, with the words "Rosemary for Remembrance".

"Careful of that cup, now," said Mrs. Hemphill. "It was your Gran's favourite."

Margaret hurriedly put it down, but it was too near Evelyn's elbow. Her little cousin moved and accidentally brushed it off the table.

"Now look what you've done," Mrs. Hemphill went to sweep up the broken bits. "Well, well! What can you expect of children? Good thing your Gran didn't see that."

Margaret and Evelyn looked at each other with startled eyes.

What if Gran-gran did see them? The two cousins wandered into the hall. Gran-gran's home looked the same as ever: Chairs of dark wood, carved with elaborate designs of flowers and urns, with uncomfortably hard seats. A window with exotic flowers—tropical violets and spider plants. A curio cabinet with a collection of arrowheads, a stone axe, and plaster figures of strange gods brought back by an ancestor from the Orient. On the wall hung a sampler, embroidered by Gran-gran, showing a willow-tree weeping over a tombstone, and the motto, "In hope of Blessed Resurrection."

People did rise from the dead. Sometimes.

Evelyn started up the stairs, hanging on to the carved wooden banister, and climbed up two feet to a step. "Don't go up there!" Margaret called.

"Why not?"

"That's where Gran-gran's room is." Margaret had been taken each week to see her grandmother after Gran-gran got sick. Holding her mother's hand, she would walk upstairs slowly, not really wishing to see the old, old lady. She was over 80, her mother told her. The first visits were not so bad. Gran-gran was sitting up, with a little smile. Her sunken eyes seemed to recognize Margaret, and she would vaguely reach out and squeeze her hand. But sometimes she would seem to be asleep, though her eyes were open, lying there, her white hair scanty, with patches of pink skin showing through. Her mouth would be half open with a little dribble of spit flowing out. Sometimes, when they visited, Gran-gran would be groaning softly, "Oh-oh-oh," and thrash her head from side to side, not looking at Margaret and her mother at all.

The last visit was the worst. Mother had said, "Here's Margaret, Granny, here's your granddaughter." Gran-gran's face was distorted, her mouth twisted, and her head rolled back and forth on the pillow. She had held up a knotted, skeletal hand between her and Margaret and cried, "No, no, Get away! Don't come near me!"

Margaret had run out of the room. After that, she wouldn't go in the room when her mother went to visit Gran-gran.

Evelyn was at the top of the stairs. "What's in these rooms?" she asked. Living farther away, she had never seen Gran when she was sick. Margaret followed slowly to the upper hall. There was a shadowy feeling about going near Gran-gran's room. The hall was dark. All the shades in the house had been pulled down. "That's what we do when someone dies," her mother had told her. Gran's house was gloomy anyway with dark wood mouldings, old fashioned lights with glass shades shaped like flower petals, and old pictures on the walls of churches, ruined buildings, and some dead pheasants. Also at the end of the hall between two windows was a painting of an old man with a long beard, a frown, and deep-set eyes. He wore a tall black hat with a wide brim. Evelyn stood in front of it. "He's a witch!" she said.

"You mean a wizard," Margaret corrected. "He's Grandpa, and he died years and years ago, before I was born."

From the edge of the drawn window shade, a thin spear of sunlight fell on the old man's eyes, making them glitter, as if he were staring at them. Evelyn grabbed Margaret's arm. "He heard us. He's mad at us!" she whispered.

All the room doors were shut. Margaret opened one. It was the bathroom. The light was dim, but she still made out an old wooden-enclosed bathtub, long and square. It reminded her of her grandmother's coffin. Water dripped from a faucet, *plop, plop, plop*. Over the basin, Margaret and Evelyn looked at their own faces, peering out of the cracked mirror from a world of shadows.

The girls tiptoed out into the hall, but in spite of trying to be quiet, their footsteps made the floor squeak and they hurried to the next room. The door swung open slowly. In the dimness there was absolutely nothing. A bare wood floor, no furniture, the windows with the shades pulled down. Some dust on the floor, with marks of footsteps in the dust. From the windows came a low whine as if something were trying to get in.

In the hall again, they heard Mrs. Hemphill downstairs, humming, the clash of dishes as she put them in the sink, then her footsteps back and forth. Downstairs seemed a different world, filled with ordinary life. Upstairs was half-dark and mostly empty.

"Let's go down," Evelyn whispered.

Margaret was afraid, but when she felt fear, she was compelled to face it. She could not turn her back on what made her afraid.

"Come on," she said. "We haven't seen the other rooms."

The next door opened into a study or office. There was a desk and bookshelves along the wall, and a 12-month calendar hung near the desk. The calendar had symbols on it, made out of stars, a different picture for each month: a raging bull, a horned goat, a crab, a scorpion like a lobster with a long tail. On the windowsill was a row of potted geraniums, all dried up, with brown leaves. Their long stems lay like arms reaching out, and there was a strong, pungent, decayed plant smell.

"I don't like this room," whispered Evelyn.

The last door was Gran-gran's. Margaret approached it slowly. She did not want to go in but her fear forced her to put her hand on the door-knob. What if her grandmother was still inside? What if she was in bed, sitting up? Gran-gran would cry, *"Get away, get out!"* What if the coffin, carried out of the house earlier, had been empty, and her grandmother was in her room, waiting to catch her and scold her for breaking her favourite cup? What if she reached out and grabbed her with her claw-like hand to shake her....

Margaret opened the door, Evelyn just behind her. At first they could see nothing. The room was dim with the shades pulled down and heavy curtains pulled across the windows.

Evelyn pushed in against her, more because she didn't want to be left alone than because she wanted to go in.

Their grandmother sat in a chair, a narrow beam of light on her face. She looked right at them. Margaret froze, paralysed. She could not move, scream, or even breathe. She felt Evelyn's body behind her begin to shake. Their grandmother's face was not pale and grey as she had been when lying in bed. Her cheeks were firmer, and were a pale pink colour. Her white hair was thick, and piled in a chignon on top of her head.

Margaret breathed, "Gran?" In her amazement, she forgot to be afraid. She stepped into the room, Evelyn beside her.

Evelyn began, "You're not in the box! They didn't take you away!"

Their grandmother didn't move, or seem to hear them.

They ran to Gran-gran. The air from the open bedroom door shifted the curtains, letting in more sunlight. Brown wrapping paper covered her grandmother's arms and body. Above Gran's head and around her sides was a gilded frame, which was set on an armchair.

Confused, Evelyn said, "Take off the paper so she can walk!"

Like a person coming out of a dream and not sure what was real, Margaret carefully pulled the wrapping paper from her grandmother's body. She soon saw the whole frame, and quickly looked in back to see that there was nothing there, just the flat stretched canvas in the armchair.

"It's Gran, in a picture," Margaret told her little cousin.

"Is she here, or is she in the box?" Evelyn could not grasp what she was seeing. The picture showed Gran-gran sitting in a chair like one of the carved wood chairs downstairs. She was wearing a lovely flowered dress, and a necklace of green jade. She was holding something in her hands—an album—and in the album on the left-hand page was an oval picture of a smiling two-year-old with curls around her baby face. Written above it was, "My darling granddaughter, Margaret."

"That's me when I was little!" Margaret told her cousin.

On the right-hand page was another oval picture of a baby with fat cheeks and bright eyes, and above it was written, "My darling granddaughter, Evelyn."

"That's you, when you were a baby," Margaret said.

Gran-Gran in the picture was smiling tenderly at the photos.

"Why, she likes us!" said Margaret.

Evelyn reached out with a careful finger and touched Gran-gran's hand. The hand was plump and not claw-like at all. "She's pretty," Evelyn said.

Margaret wanted to kiss Gran's cheek. But she knew it was silly to kiss a painted picture. Instead, she kissed her own fingers, and touched them to Gran's cheek. Why had she thought Gran might reach out and grab her? Of course, she loved Gran and Gran loved her. They stood looking at the picture for a minute, then turned away. Margaret shut the door behind her, and they went downstairs.

Mrs. Hemphill regarded them carefully when they entered the kitchen. "And what have you two been up to?"

Margaret felt very calm. "Oh, nothing."

"Why don't you girls go out in the garden and play?" Mrs. Hemphill suggested. "It's not good to be too quiet and shut up inside when you are young."

In the back yard, Margaret and Evelyn sat on each side of a wooden swing-seat and made it sway back and forth. The image of Gran with a twisted face, and a skeletal hand, crying, "*Get out!*" had faded away. Gran-gran was a lady in a flowered dress sitting upright, with abundant white hair in a chignon, looking lovingly at pictures of her granddaughters.

~~~***~~~

Who's The Old Hag?

Russell Barton

The attempt to move fails. You're paralysed. Breathing, an effort, is controlled by another. A woman's voice, old, crackled, whispers. The words are clear. "Now you are hot and sweaty, your heart will stop, breath shall leave you. Death and darkness must surely follow. Let me be your companion, your guide in the hereafter."

Breathing stops. Is suffocation to be your fate? Eyelids, after a supreme effort, open halfway. A grey pockmarked hag's face hovers above, her eyes staring maliciously into yours. You recognise a nightmare and desperately try, in your mind, to rock back and forth hoping to generate motion and wakefulness. You emit a stifled gasp. At last you sense a reach into consciousness. Cold air and physical awareness waft over your mind and body.

The hag's face shrinks away but her sinewy hands grasp at your shoulders. Your scream reverberates throughout the hotel.

Her face retreats further towards the darkness, your eyes open wide. The wraith, gliding towards a dark corner, dissolves into an ominous shadowy form. Awakening and speedily sitting up, you clumsily try to activate the bedside lamp but fail.

It takes a few seconds before hotel guests, alarmed by the scream, arrive outside your room. They bang on the door.

"Who is in there? Are you OK?"

You attempt to explain, wanting to say, "Yes, thanks, just a bad dream," but no sound comes forth. Unable to communicate you try the door. The handle won't turn. Is it locked? Puzzled, you push. Now you are outside the room slowly moving along the hotel corridor. Guests scream and run. A priest blocks your path. He is holding out a crucifix at chest level. "Be gone, be gone foul creature!"

You try to tell him that he has the wrong person, and turn to point at the wraith in the room's interior but the door is closed. You feel faint, objects are blurring. In the distance you see a bright light.

The commanding voice of the priest asks, "Who are you? What is your name?" Somehow his questions demand a response and they power your voice.

"Matthew." It sounds laboured and strange.

"Matthew, you no longer belong here. It's time to leave, to pass on. Have courage. Now, I command you, Matthew, enter the tunnel. Go to the light at the end."

~~~***~~~

The Skeleton without a Skull
Maida Follini

I fought for family and for farm
Against the French when they did swarm.
Now here at home my bones do rest
But where my head is, who can guess?

Living next door to a graveyard may seem gloomy to some, but for Marjory, the Old Cemetery in Dartmouth was her familiar play yard from her earliest years. She loved to walk among gravestones that stood high above the harbour, looking out to sea. The oldest burials were not marked. A tablet remembered, "Many Mi'kmaq and early settlers are buried in this place." Later graves had a variety of tombstones. Marjory petted the marble lambs on the children's graves, and looked up into the eyes of carved angels whose wings spread protectively over family plots. Some of the plots contained tombs like small stone houses, with pillared porches, where Marjory could play house, picking flowers to decorate sombre pillars. Other plots contained English settler families, with tall stone blocks for the parents, and a row of smaller stones for the children.

The quiet children under the sod were her friends, and she brought wild flowers to decorate their graves, or special things like a blue jay's feather or a shining white stone.

Sometimes Marjory wandered over the mossy turf, reading the inscriptions and trying to make out the meaning of the carvings and mottoes on the stones:

Praying hands and "Be Thou Also Ready"
"Rest Eternal" and "In Peace"

One inscription presented a mystery:

"I fought for family and for farm
Against the French when they did swarm.
Now here at home my bones do rest,
Where my head lies, none can guess."

Often and often, Marjory returned to this stone, one of the oldest in the cemetery. She had brushed the moss away to read the name:

Henry Ainsworth
Born Norwich, England 1720
Died Dartmouth, Nova Scotia 1749

Marjory imagined the bones buried six feet under the earth: feet, legs, ribs, arms—but no head! What had happened to Henry's head? Suppose he woke up on Judgement Day, and found he had no head? Marjory wondered if a headless person could enter Heaven. How would St. Peter know it was Henry?

On the thirtieth of October, Marjory gathered especially large bunches of goldenrod and purple asters, and placed them on Henry's grave. Tomorrow night was Hallowe'en, when ghosts were supposed to walk, and spirits rose from the grave to have one night when they could range about and celebrate before returning underground. And she wanted everyone to know that someone cared for Henry Ainsworth, even though he had no head.

"There, you're not forgotten," she said to Henry.

"Who are you talking to?" A boy's voice startled her.

Marjory stared. "What are you doing here?" It was Ned, a buddy from her fifth grade class. Ned lived the next street over from her and their mothers were friends.

"Checking out the graveyard," said Ned. "Some of the guys are daring each other to do a ghost walk here, tomorrow night, and I thought I'd get here first and scare them! What are *you* doing here? Aren't you afraid of a graveyard?"

"Of course not," scoffed Marjory. "Why, I come here all the time!"

"Who were you talking to?" Ned asked again.

"Henry." Marjory pointed to the stone. "I tell him I'm sorry for him because he has no head."

"No head?" Ned came closer and studied the grave marker. He read, "'But where my head lies, none can guess.' Say, that's weird! How come he doesn't have a head?"

"It's a mystery," Marjory replied. "At least, I don't know."

"Say, that would be scary. To see a skeleton without a head." Ned thought for a moment, then his eyes lit up. "That would make a good costume for Hallowe'en! But I wonder what his story is."

Marjory showed Ned around the cemetery, pointing out stones she was familiar with. But both of them kept returning to Henry Ainsworth's plot, the man without a head. Marjory patted the gravestone. "Don't worry, Henry, we're your friends even if you don't have a head!" Then she jumped back. "Something moved!" she exclaimed. "Under my feet!"

Ned stared at the turf covering the grave. He said in a low tone, "Did you hear that rumbling sound? Something's under there."

"Of course," Marjory replied, with a nervous laugh. "Henry's there!"

"Do you think he heard us?"

"He might be sensitive about having no head." Marjory took care not to step on the grass over the grave again.

"If only we could find out where it was, we could get it back for him," Ned suggested. "I could ask my grandfather about it. He knows a lot of early history."

Was there a movement atop the grave? Both children stared at the grass. "I thought it rippled a little," said Marjory.

"Probably just the wind," Ned offered, but he was quiet as they turned to go home.

"If you find out anything from your grandfather, tell me in school tomorrow," said Marjory.

The next morning, Marjory hurried over to Ned, who was standing in line in front of the school, waiting for the doors to open.

"Did you find out about… you know?" she whispered, so the other kids wouldn't hear.

"Gramp told me the whole story! It's wild!" Ned's eyes gleamed with excitement.

"Tell me."

"I can't right now. The bell's going to ring. I'll tell you at lunch."

At lunch, she managed to snag a spot in the window alcove in the corner of the classroom. Ned sauntered over to join her, trying to appear casual. But as soon as he sat down and opened his lunch box, Marjory cried out, "Tell! Tell!"

"It was Indians! In the Seven Years War! Henry was cutting wood. He and five other men. Some Indians rushed out of the forest and Henry was killed!"

"But why no head?"

"Gramp thinks the Mi'kmaq may have taken it away. He said the French rewarded the Indians for every Englishman they killed or captured. They scalped some others, and took one man prisoner. They must have cut off Henry's head to show the French in order to get the reward."

"Ugh!" Marjory made a face.

"Well, the English did the same thing, Gramp said. They paid a bounty for every Indian scalp the English took."

"I wouldn't want to carry around an old head."

"Maybe they dropped it on the way home," Ned speculated. Ned and Marjory looked at each other, and then down at their lunch boxes. Neither felt much like eating anymore. Ned had an image of a head carried by its hair, blood dripping from its neck. In Marjory's mind, she saw the lost head, flung down on the hill above the harbour, and rolling, rolling down to the shore with a ghastly smile on its face.

When lunch was over, the teacher, Miss Primrose, smiled at her restless class. "Come on, get your coats on. We're going on a field trip!" she announced. "The Parent-Teacher Organization has arranged with the Museum down the block for you to attend a special children's Hallowe'en program."

Within a few minutes, the fifth graders, all 26 of them, were marching two by two to the Alderney Museum. The entrance had a large banner: "Hallowe'en exhibit: Ghosts, Goblins, and Haunts." A museum instructor led them to a darkened maze set up in the galleries, with phosphorescent stepping stones for the children to follow. There were black "spider web" curtains they had to lift to go between the galleries.

The first gallery had enlarged models of insects displayed on the walls: praying mantises, cicadas, wasps, and dragonflies. There was also a remote-controlled spider. The instructor let the children take turns using the control stick to make it crawl across the floor.

The next gallery had a mock jail set up in a corner, and life-size "stocks" to punish early settlers who had a run-in with the authorities. "You could be put in the stocks for not attending church on Sunday," said the instructor. "And when ships came in, the jail would fill up, because sailors would often be jailed for public drunkenness."

While several classmates vied for the chance to be put in the "stocks", or locked in the "jail", Ned and Marjory peered around the door to the next gallery. Paper skeletons hung on the walls beside charts naming all their bones. A large glass case was in the centre of the room. Marjory hung over the glass. "Ned! Look!" Ned hurried over. Staring back at them from under the glass were the black empty eye-sockets of a human skull!

"We don't know whose skull is in this case." The Museum instructor moved to the display case. "It was dug up recently by a construction crew. The experts who looked at it say it is a man's skull and that it must be very old, because it was under layers and layers of soil."

The fifth graders crowded around. "Was he murdered? Who killed him?" someone asked.

Miss Primrose said, "How do you know he was murdered? Maybe he died of disease."

"No, Ma'am," said the instructor. He pulled on a pair of white gloves, unlocked the case, and carefully turned the skull so the class could see the back of the head. The back of the skull had been split and there was a hatchet head still embedded in the bone. "We think he was one of the early settlers. During the Seven Years War, there were many skirmishes between the English, and the French and their Indian allies. Many Englishmen and many natives were killed, right here in Dartmouth.

"The skull was found right near here, at the bottom of the hill, near the shore. So he was probably an early settler or a soldier in the Halifax area. But the strange thing is we didn't find any of his other bones or anything else, like a belt or uniform buttons that we could have identified him with."

Ned and Marjory stood back from the crowd. They exchanged slightly startled and meaningful looks, but didn't say a word.

Later, on the way back to school, Ned was excited. "It must be Henry's skull!"

Marjory agreed. "No bones were found with him because they weren't there!"

As school let out, many of the kids were calling back and forth about Hallowe'en:

"What are you going to be, tonight?"

"I'm going to be a witch!"

"A zombie!"

A bunch of boys were calling out to each other. "I'll meet you for trick or treating!"

"You're scared! Bet you won't show up!"

"I'll be at the Old Cemetery, but I won't see you! You'll be home hiding under your bed!"

"Dare you to walk through the whole grounds!"

"Double-dare!"

Marjory asked Ned, "Are you going to the graveyard to scare those guys?"

"I'm going to wear an all-black outfit," Ned said, "and glue a paper skeleton on it, but I'll take off the skull! I'll be the skeleton without a head! That ought to shock them."

"I'll come with you. I'll be a ghost in a white sheet."

The problem of how to stay out late was solved by each of them telling their parents that they were going to a Hallowe'en party at the other's house. Neither took bags to hold candy with them.

"It's tricks for me tonight, not treats," said Ned, when they met up later.

Marjory nodded. Marjory was carrying a sheet, and when she put it over her head, she could see out of the holes she had cut for the eyes. The sheet draped down over her, so that nothing showed except her shoes.

Ned's white paper skeleton contrasted quite well against his black outfit, and he wore a black ski-mask over his head so that it would not be seen in the dark.

In the Old Cemetery, they hid behind Henry Ainsworth's stone to wait for the boys from school. At first, it was scarcely dark enough, but as the night closed in Ned and Marjory peered around the stone every few minutes to see if the boys were coming. They could see the other graves, lit by faint moonlight—the little children with lambs, the carved angel with outstretched wings. It was too dark to read the inscription on Henry's grave, but they could recall it without having to read it.

"Where my head lies, none can guess!" said Marjory. "But we know, don't we?"

"Right there in the Museum! They say that dead men who lose their bones constantly seek to find them," said Ned. "I wonder if Henry's skeleton…."

"Hush," shushed Marjory. She had heard something.

"Are the guys coming?" whispered Ned.

But the creaking noise did not come from the cemetery entrance. It came from the other side of Henry's stone. Marjory peered around. Something funny was going on. The earth of the plot was rippling, the way it does when a mole is digging under a lawn. Marjory grasped Ned's arm.

"What is it?" hissed Ned.

"Look!"

Not only was the grass heaving, but a crack opened between the grass and Henry's tombstone. Ned and Marjory froze. Marjory's heart beat fast as a long bony finger reached up out of the crack, followed by the whole hand, and then an arm-bone. As the children held their breaths, a whole skeleton clambered out of the narrow crevice. There was a rib cage, hip bones, long thigh bones and lower legs, and feet with big bony toes. But as the skeleton stood up, they saw above the rib cage and spine—nothing! No head! The spine ended at the neck vertebrae.

Ned and Marjory huddled together behind Henry's stone, too terrified to run. They hoped the skeleton didn't see them. Did you die if a skeleton touched you?

Henry's skeleton took a few steps, but his stance appeared wobbly. Ned and Marjory saw spaces between the bones. There was no flesh and no tendons to hold the bones together. Only a pale phosphorescent light, like an electric gleam or a magnetic pulse, joined the bones.

"He's going to seek his head!" gasped Ned. "I told you dead men look for their bones!"

As they watched, Henry's skeleton set off from his grave along a cemetery path. Where the path turned, however, Henry went straight ahead into a ditch and fell down in a clatter.

"He can't see!" exclaimed Marjory. "His eyes are in the skull! He's blind!" Impulsively, she stood up and ran around the tombstone to follow the skeleton.

"Wait! Marjory!" Ned followed her. Marjory ran along the path to where the bones were piled in a ditch. They had come apart, but under Marjory's astonished gaze, they joined together again, like drops of mercury, pulled by some secret force. Within half a minute, Henry's skeleton stood up and tried to find his way out of the ditch.

"Oh, the poor thing!" cried Marjory. She reached out her hand and took the bony fingers in her grasp. She winced at the coldness of the bone, but she couldn't leave Henry's blind skeleton to stumble into ditches. "Come on, this way!" She guided him back to the path. "Ned, come on! We have to help him find his skull!"

Ned only hesitated a second. He wasn't going to let Marjory see he was afraid of the skeleton. He reached for Henry's other hand. The two children, with Henry between them, took the path that led to the cemetery's entrance. Ned found he wasn't afraid any longer. It was quite like helping his granddad to his rocking chair on the porch. Henry's hands loosely grasped Ned's and Ned helped steer him along the path. As they approached the cemetery gate, a piercing shriek rang out, followed by cries of, "A Skeleton!"

"Two Skeletons!"

"And a Ghost!"

They caught a glimpse of a group of boys, turning and running for dear life in all directions away from the cemetery.

"The guys!" said Ned, and he began to laugh. "They saw Henry, and they thought I was a skeleton, too!"

"I guess I made a good ghost." Marjory grinned. "Henry, you sure made them run!"

Henry's bony hands pulled at them. His one purpose was to find his head!

"Maybe we should try to hide him," Marjory suggested. "He'll likely scare the whole street!" But the skeleton insisted on walking right on down the street, and they had to go with him to keep him from running into lamp-posts and crashing into garbage pails.

Halfway down the street to the Museum, a group of costumed kids approached, running, whooping, and hollering. They were ringing doorbells and collecting treats. As they came closer, Marjory and Ned expected them to scream and run away, but surprisingly, nothing of the sort happened. The costumed witches, pirates, and zombies paid little attention to the two skeletons and the ghost, except one girl who said, "Great costumes!" as she rushed by.

"I can't believe it!" Marjory exclaimed. "They think he's just someone dressed up as a skeleton!"

"Better costume than mine," laughed Ned, studying Henry's detached limbs, held together by little gleams of light.

At the Museum, they had to help Henry climb the steps, lest he fall over backwards. Once they reached the top, Marjory groaned, "Of course, the doors are locked!" But that did not stop the skeleton. Without even trying to open the doors, he just slid through them without breaking them, like water through a sieve, leaving the two children outside, amazed.

As Henry disappeared into the galleries, Ned and Marjory were left open-mouthed. Was this really happening? They were not left to question long. First, they heard a crash of glass. Then bony footsteps *click-clacked* as Henry returned, holding his skull in his hands. He came out through the door the same way he went in. "Sliding through the atoms," said Ned, who was a science freak.

Once outside the Museum, the skeleton lifted the skull, and put it back on his neck vertebrae, where it seemed to fit. "As if made for him," said Marjory. Ned noticed the hatchet sticking out of the back of Henry's skull as the skeleton walked on his own down the Museum steps. He needed no guidance this time, and seemed to know his way back to the cemetery. He didn't pay any attention to Ned and Marjory, for which they were thankful. They weren't sure that a skeleton, however indebted to them for their help, might react. In fairy stories, the "Little People" were supposed to entice mortals down into their barrows underground. Neither wanted his bony hands to pull them into his grave.

Following at a safe distance, they turned into the cemetery, just in time to see Henry reach his tombstone, sit down on the edge of the opening, insert his long bony limbs into the grave, and quickly drop completely underground, and out of sight. Then from the grave-hole, two skeletal hands reached up, and for a minute, Marjory thought with a shudder that he was going to climb out of the grave again. *If he wants me to take him home*, Marjory thought, *I don't think Mother would like it*. But no, he simply reached up, grabbed the turf, and closed it with his bony fingers, like a blanket.

Then there was nothing but the unbroken ground, and nothing more to see. All was quiet, and still, as if he had never appeared.

Marjory and Ned waited a while in silence. The town clock bell chimed 12 times. It was midnight. Hallowe'en was over and All

Saints' Day was beginning. Ghosts, goblins and skeletons were now supposed to be at rest.

"Well!" said Marjory.

"Well!" responded Ned.

The whole episode left them speechless for many minutes. "Should we tell?" Marjory finally asked.

"They wouldn't believe us," said Ned.

Back at their own homes, when their parents asked them if they had a good time, neither said much. *Must be tired*, the parents thought, and hurried them to bed.

The next morning, both children woke believing that the previous night's events couldn't have happened.

But the evidence showed otherwise. The skull was gone from the Museum, where the glass case had been broken into. No one ever found out who had "stolen" the skull.

Except, of course, Marjory and Ned. They knew it hadn't been stolen at all, just reclaimed by its rightful owner.

In the cemetery, no one but Marjory and Ned noticed the inscription on Henry Ainsworth's grave had changed:

I fought for family and for farm
Against the French when they did swarm
For long my bones were not complete
But now united I can sleep.

~~~***~~~

</div>

Fate

Diane Losier

"Meep! Meep! Meep! Meep!" The alarm called everyone to attention. "This is not a drill! This is not a drill!"

The lower deck was rapidly filling with hot acrid smoke. He knew that something was seriously wrong. Within seconds, visibility plummeted to zero. He had to find his way to the face masks and locate one of the fresh-air intakes situated at intervals along the sides of the sub. Only trouble was, even his flashlight couldn't pierce through the thick wall of smoke enveloping him. He was completely disoriented as he felt his way through the thickening darkness. His eyes hurt, his lungs were on fire. On the verge of collapsing he yelled, "I need some air! Some air! Help!"

Josh sat bolt upright, covered in a cold sweat, his heart beating furiously. It took him a few seconds to realize he was in his bed, not on the *Nunavut*. He slowly got up and shuffled to the kitchen for a glass of water. No point in going back to bed. He knew he wouldn't sleep, so he sat at the table and lit a cigarette. Although his flashbacks happened less and less, and he had been encouraged not to dwell on them, he couldn't help recalling the events of that terrible accident.

His posting on the *HMCS Nunavut* had been part of his second, four-year commission in the Canadian Navy. They had purchased four used subs from the Royal Navy and the *Nunavut* was on its way to the port of Halifax for refitting when the incident happened.

No one had noticed the leak in one of the hatches near the conning tower. That day, the sea had been getting steadily worse. The sub was not yet fit to dive and avoid the storm. Over time she had taken on a large volume of sea water. The bigger problem, though was that the insulation around the wires in the main control panel was worn. Water falling on those cables caused a massive electrical short, leading to a fire above deck near the conning tower.

There was no flooding below, but the transformer boxes blew up and caused a second fire. The underwater decks plunged into total darkness. Billowing smoke from the fire added to the confusion.

As soon as the alarm went off, the smoke screens dropped, isolating the fire and preventing it from spreading to the rest of the sub. The crew had been trained for such an emergency. From the area farthest from the fire, a team donned their fire-fighting gear. Within minutes they were poised to douse the hot flames with jets of CO_2.

Josh had passed out before reaching the masks and fresh-air ducts. It was a lucky fluke that his buddy, Dave, having heard his cry for help, stumbled over him in the pitch dark and managed to drag him to the side of the sub. Seconds later, one member of the emergency team arrived and shared his air with Josh before taking him to safety.

In the days and weeks following the accident, Josh tried in vain not to think of that event, but in fact he had thought about it constantly. He couldn't eat, he couldn't sleep. Upon his return from that ill-fated voyage, as an engineer he was assigned to work on the refitting of the *Nunavut*. However, just the thought of stepping back on the deck of a sub filled him with nausea and dread.

The navy gave him a shore posting, with the expectation that this problem would eventually vanish. He continued to have trouble falling asleep at night and when he did, it was never for long. His buddies found him to be increasingly irritable, no longer laughing at their off-duty antics. His superior officer reported that he wasn't even fit for a desk job, as he couldn't concentrate for more than a few minutes at a time. Finally, Josh was ordered to be evaluated by the base psychologist, who diagnosed his condition as PTSD.

This diagnosis brought relief to Josh's girlfriend who had borne the brunt of those first few months. Kate was sympathetic and supportive at first, but over time his emotional aloofness and his bouts of irrational anger got the better of her. She couldn't understand why he was so angry whenever she tried to get him to talk about his experience. She kept saying he needed to "let it out". She was hurt that in spite of all her support, he never trusted her enough to share his problems. Josh started drinking more heavily. Night after night he stumbled home and got Kate out of bed when he couldn't fit the key in the lock. He found ways to pick fights with her, complaining about how she had gained weight or was getting boring; anything to relieve the agitation he felt inside. After eight months of almost constant fighting, Kate finally left. In the middle of his anguish Josh realized that he had two choices: stay on this self-destructive path or seek help. He chose the latter.

After a few months, his cognitive therapy sessions finally showed results. At each session he imagined longer portions of his frightening experience, while at the same time keeping his breathing and heartbeat in check. He joined a support group, started jogging, and quit drinking.

That was two years ago. Over time Josh's worst symptoms abated. He understood enough about his condition to realize that he had to get away from his daily routine and start afresh elsewhere. When his second commission ran out, he quit the navy. By then Kate had moved on and he was free to go anywhere. He decided to return to Cape Breton, to the town he used to visit every summer when his grandparents were still alive.

Cheticamp, with its picturesque harbour, is a small, mostly French village, on the western shore of Cape Breton. Josh's mother had been raised there and, after she had passed away, he had inherited his grandparents' old house at the edge of town. Although he couldn't speak French, it didn't take him long to fit in, as many of the childhood boys he played with were now local fishermen. Working on one of their fishing boats would have been a natural choice for Josh, but it was too soon. He decided to work for his friend, Daniel, who owned a small marina on the northern end of Cheticamp Harbour. His skills as a first-rate marine engineer soon got the attention of the locals. Eventually, Daniel offered him a partnership, to prevent him from leaving and starting a business on his own.

The life-style suited Josh well. On balmy mornings he walked the two kilometres to work, breathing in the fresh sea air. He found the pace of village life relaxing compared to the demands of military service. He kept his drinking to a couple of beers on Saturday nights, playing pool with the boys at The Doryman. Josh wasn't much of a talker, but he was well liked and increasingly respected in the community.

One late winter evening he had won another round of pool and was looking for a new challenger. To his surprise a willowy brunette smiled at him as she picked up a cue from the rack on the wall.

"Melanie Aucoin," she said, shaking his hand.

"Josh Beaton," he replied.

He was immediately drawn to her warm brown eyes and mischievous smile. The challenge was on!

It was unusual to see a female pool player. However, it soon became obvious that Melanie knew how to play pool. It didn't take long before there were a few bets going around. Josh was playing well, but he was beginning to sweat. Melanie won the first game, he won the second. The third round was neck-and-neck until his cue slipped and brushed against the 8-ball, which oh so slowly made its way into the right side pocket.

"Damn!" he said, looking up at Melanie with his lop-sided smile.

Money exchanged hands amid cheers and laughter. Josh walked up to Melanie and bowed, offering his cue, much as a defeated knight would relinquish his sword.

Melanie laughed and offered to buy him a beer.

Josh replied, "Never mind the consolation prize. Let me buy *you* a victory drink!"

Josh was surprised when Melanie finished her beer and headed for the stage. A fiddler and bass player were already setting up. He expected her to sit at the piano and was delighted when she opened a black case and pulled out a large accordion. For the next 40 minutes the place was jumping as the trio went from one lively Cajun tune to the other. Melanie kept time with her feet, occasionally flashing her bright smile his way. He was smitten.

From then on, instead of going home after work, he often ended up at her small apartment over the Acadian Restaurant. She, in turn, spent most of her weekends at his place. They explored the back roads in his Ford pick-up truck and went for long hikes in the Highlands. When summer came, Josh set up a permanent tent on Cheticamp Island, where they spent many evenings swimming in the clear cool waters. He often sat on the rocks at the end of the long sandy beach gazing at the waves glinting in the setting sun. Slowly, over time, he found himself opening up to Melanie, letting her in on his private terrors. She knew better not to push these moments of intimacy, offering an open ear and a kind heart, rather than misplaced advice.

One of the summer visitors put his Tanzer 25 up for sale and Josh decided to buy it. He had sailed with his grandfather as a boy and in no time he found his sea legs again. This was completely different from being on a submarine. He felt in control and, keeping an eye on the tides and the weather, he was no longer filled with anxiety. Instead, the open sea gave him an exhilarating sense of freedom.

When she wasn't working at the local hospital, Melanie often accompanied him on these outings. She proudly stepped aboard the *Melanie Jane* and was learning the ropes. At first she sat back and watched Josh handle the boat on his own. She screamed with equal parts fear and excitement when the boat heeled in high winds. Eventually though, she learned to hold the tiller while Josh brought down the mainsail and to pull in the jib while tacking.

One Sunday late in June, Josh headed out on his own. Once out of the harbour he headed south. The wind was light and gulls followed him offshore on this bright sunny afternoon. He intended to sail to Inverness if the wind was favourable. He didn't quite make it, although he had a great afternoon's sail. By 4 p.m. he pulled in his jib and tacked on a course heading back to Cheticamp. He noticed a bank of fog coming in from the southwest and hoped to reach port before it overtook him. An hour later the wind died down and he was enveloped in a thick, grey fog. Out of nowhere, a big swell tipped his sailboat off course. By the time she was back upright, he had lost all sense of direction.

He chose not to turn on his motor, afraid to waste precious fuel going in the wrong direction. There was nothing to do but sit tight and hope for the fog to lift. After a while he tried to get his bearing by listening to the waves crashing on the shore, but the sea was silent. He became more and more alarmed as thick fog swirled around him. He started gasping for air, his heart beat loudly in his chest. He tried to control the mounting anxiety brought on by his feeling of complete disorientation.

Josh had one hand on the tiller when he thought he saw something coming towards him. He peered into the thick fog and saw what looked like the outline of a large fishing boat. The image sharpened as it approached. Minutes later a 42-foot Cape Islander appeared out of the fog and turned alongside the *Melanie Jane*. He was surprised to see a woman in her late sixties at the helm. She was dressed in a fisherman's slicker, and her wild grey hair framed a well-worn face. She didn't say a word but beckoned him to follow her. As the boat went on ahead of him, Josh read the neatly painted name, *Marion Rose.*

He quickly turned on his engine and followed from about 50 feet astern. The woman never looked back and kept on going at a steady pace. They motored on for about 45 minutes until the *Marion Rose* slowed down to let Josh approach. The woman then turned to Josh's boat and pointed to starboard. By then the fog had started to dissipate and he recognized the entrance to Cheticamp Harbour. He turned toward shore, expecting the other boat to do the same, but when he looked back the *Marion Rose* had vanished.

At the pub later that night, Josh recounted his adventure.

"Was she wearing a captain's cap?" asked Terry.

"Yes, as a matter of fact she was."

"Well," replied his friend," you were rescued by the 'Captain's Widow'. You're some lucky bastard!"

That evening Josh learned that in the early 60s, Captain John Campbell, a local fisherman, had often gone out to sea with his wife. She was a legend in the area, a strong hardy woman. One day in 1964 she stayed ashore while her husband took the boat out. A severe squall came upon him unexpectedly. They found his boat but his body was never found. The next season the Captain's wife began to take the *Marion Rose* out on her own. People were concerned but she knew what she was doing. One day in late August, a few people saw her go out to sea, even though they were forecasting the worst storm of the season. They never saw her or the *Marion Rose* again.

Once in a while there would be another tale of how some lost tourist was shown the way back home by following her ghostly boat. Over the years her legend grew and she became known as "The Captain's Widow".

Josh didn't put much stock in these ghostly stories. He'd heard enough spooky yarns during his late-night shifts on the *Nunavut* than to take all this seriously. Still, stories his grandfather had told gave him enough respect for the supernatural to keep an open mind.

Things were working out well for Josh. He owned his own home, he had a great job and he was deeply in love. In the fall, he planned to take a trip to Quebec City with Melanie and ask her to marry him.

Josh loved those days in late September, when the warm air and the honeyed light made him feel summer would go on forever.

Once again he had taken his boat out toward Inverness. It was early evening as he approached the narrow gut at the north end of Cheticamp Harbour. The sea had been getting steadily worse and he was relieved to be so close to home. He didn't see the empty oil drum bobbing up and down in the rising swells. The *Melanie Jane* hit the oil drum head on. The bow shot up and the boat flipped on its side. The wildly swerving boom hit Josh on the side of the head and he was thrown into the turbulent sea. Dazed and gasping for air, he flailed in the water, trying to get his bearing. He was confused; images of impenetrable smoke flashed in his mind. He experienced the same burning lungs, the same desperate need for air. As his body was violently tossed by the crashing waves, Josh lost consciousness.

It was dark when he awoke. He was lying face down on a shale beach. It took him a while to remember what had happened. Painfully, he raised himself to a standing position and looked around. It was such a relief when he saw the village lights quite close by. He wrapped his arms around himself to keep from shaking, and he stumbled over rocks and seaweed, finally reaching the edge of the village. He was just below the deck of The Doryman. With a final effort he pulled himself up the steep grassy slope and reached the back entrance.

It was a fine Saturday night and the place was full. Two of his buddies were playing pool along the left wall. Josh was overjoyed to see Melanie talking to Terry at the bar. They had planned to meet there for supper after her shift. She looked his way briefly. He waved, expecting her to wave in return. He was surprised when she turned her back to him and ordered another beer from the bartender. Josh took a few steps forward, more and more puzzled that no one was looking his way, no one was coming to help.

It was then that he noticed an old man sitting in the corner booth. The old man raised his glass at him and smiled. Josh was taken aback by how much the old fella looked like his grandfather. Then his attention was caught by a woman sitting alone at a side table. He could only see the back of her frizzy grey hair. She was wearing a black slicker, and a captain's hat rested on the table beside her. He slowly walked around and stood in front of her. She looked him straight in the eye and, smiling, beckoned him to sit beside her. At that moment Josh's legs gave way and he slumped to the floor. Before falling into oblivion he had a moment of utter clarity.

~~~***~~~

The Séance
Russell Barton

"When I die, you get this, love. Not that you'll ever use it." Lilly Coker, who I had known for as long as I could remember, pulled an Ouija board from an old, ornate Captain's trunk. "Do you remember Mrs. Grimes who held séances during the war at your family's house? She always used my Ouija board. This one." Lilly pointed at the board and then set it on the table. I recognised it. "Oh! Lest I forget." She pulled a crystal glass from the trunk and placed it, bottom up, in the centre of the board. Smiling, she looked at me. "Fancy a whirl?"

"No, thanks." I was helping her pack for her move to an old folk's condo in Blackheath; she waitressed in our café for many years when I was very young. The café was at the front of the kitchen and the family dining room at the rear. This arrangement made it possible for the café's waitresses to occasionally serve meals to family and guests. I always regarded her as family.

"You and your Uncle Ted and that bloomin' dog gave us quite a fright at one of Mrs. Grimes's séances."

"I remember. Everyone panicked in the dark. Mrs. Grimes hoped to communicate with the dead, especially her son, Michael, shortly after his destroyer was torpedoed in the Atlantic."

"Yes, but others in England, your relatives included, wanted to contact the loved ones they lost in the war. But whew! What a panic when the séance got out of control."

I grinned. "Even now I remember the screams."

Lilly carefully wrapped a cloth around the board and returned it to the trunk.

"It's a nice crystal. I think I'll keep it out for use at the condominium." We lapsed into silence for a few minutes, Lilly, sorting and packing, but both of us thinking about the frightening encounter with the supernatural that happened one evening early in 1944.

On the occasion of the séance, my family and their guest of honour, Mrs. Grimes, family friend and medium, settled around the dining room table drinking tea or sipping sherry while waiting to be served dinner. Even Uncle Raymond, a medical student, attended because he had been a close friend of Mrs. Grimes's son, Michael.

Suddenly, Mrs. Grimes's cup fell into its saucer. Her hand thrust forward as if to fend off a confrontation. "No, no, not yet! Can't you see, we're drinking tea? Come back later, Dearie, when I'm having my trance." She placed the cup and saucer on the table remarking, "Oh, they can be so impatient. You have to let them know when you're ready." Family and friends sat in an awkward silence for a few moments. The air raid sirens went off. "Ignore them," said Mrs. Grimes. "Our friends up there are already telling us that we'll be safe for tonight."

"Well, that's reassuring," remarked Grandma. "Let's carry on then. I'll set up Lilly's Ouija board on the smaller oak table. We can move from the dining table to it when Mrs. Grimes begins the séance." She moved over to a round oak table, next to our family dining area, and set up for consultations with the spirits.

Quickly, the waitresses, using their backs, pushed open the frosted glass door from the kitchen to the dining room and backed in with trays carrying hot bowls of soup and tureens filled with potatoes and steaming cabbage. Giggling, turning to approach the dinner table, they negotiated their way between the candles in the flickering light, and set down the trays.

"Did you get a bet on the grand national, love?" Lilly directed the question at my Grandfather as she loaded plates with food.

"Mr. Sims took it on the phone. I put five pounds to win on Hot Toy. We'll see if Mrs. Grimes's last consultation with the spirits pays off."

"Now, darling," responded Mrs. Grimes, who had just wriggled her enormous self into place next to Grandmother. "They judge horses like we do. There's nothing special about their ability to predict a winner." She set a small, red, battery powered light on the card table. Someone switched out the overhead lights. Combined with the candles, the red light gave the room an eerie presence.

"Ere 'ang on ta this, love." Lilly handed out plates loaded with vegetables to the adults. "Well, I put a quid on Hoof Hearted."

"Nice to hear you using your H's for a change! Got a tip straight from the horse's arse did ya?" Grandfather roared with laughter at his joke.

"Billy," uttered Grandmother disapprovingly.

"Gawd, no! Young 'arry 'ere told me it was a winner. And you know he picked last year's wiv 20-20," Lilly replied, ignoring Grandfather.

"Uhh uhh…" Grandmother, open mouthed, pointed to a cup rising from the table; its shadow from the candlelight flickered on the wall.

"Bleedin 'ell." Lilly dropped a plate on the floor and fled to a corner of the dining room.

The cup twisted erratically as it ascended, a trace of white cotton thread glittered in the candle light. It was above Uncle Ted, who had a benign smile on his face. Mrs. Grimes went into a trance, eyes turned upwards, lips flapping, jaw quivering, her puffed cheeks turning gun metal grey.

"Be gone, be gone, we're not ready," she commanded. The cup descended. Ted, still smiling, reached up and gently, with one hand, guided it back into its saucer.

"Good thing my tea hadn't been poured," he snickered.

Mrs. Grimes hastily emerged from her trance. "Betty," she addressed Grandmother. "How can I be expected to make contact with children present?"

"I'm not a child," Ted retorted. "I am almost old enough to die for my country."

"Ted, here's sixpence. When dinner is finished, look after Harry upstairs until his bedtime. Oh! And take Winston, too." Winston, who lay on the carpet, whimpered and pricked up his ears at the mention of his name. Grandmother handed over the coin, which Ted happily pocketed.

After dinner, Ted and I left with Winston and retired to the box room. Carefully we laid out the track to Uncle Ted's treasured Hornby OO clockwork train set.

"You can be Paddington Station." This required that I stand with one foot on either side of the track and pretend to be a railway station, an unsatisfying solution for my participation. I quickly tired of standing over the tracks.

"Let me wind it up?" I inserted the key into the side of the clockwork engine and wound until it was too hard to turn. The locomotive looked convincingly real. It was painted olive-green with black trim and resembled a turn of the century steam engine. Wheels ready to spin, I carefully placed the engine on the track. Uncle Ted had improvised a small bellows above the wheels so that when they turned they inflated the bellows, activating a horn that sounded like an owl's hoot. It performed erratically.

"Will the engine's horn work?" I was disappointed because so far it had failed to hoot.

"Yes, in a minute, but the engine has to make more circuits before the bellows inflate fully. Then the horn will sound." The locomotive efficiently made its way around the track.

Winston's eyes followed. After several circuits, he placed his paw on the rails blocking the engine's progress. The clockwork locomotive struck him and clambered up his leg, its mechanism tracked into his shaggy black fur. Yelping, he fled, hoping to leave the locomotive behind. It didn't cooperate. It wound more fur into its interior mechanisms. Uttering a tormented howl, Winston raced down the stairs with Uncle Ted and me in hot pursuit. He sought refuge in the dining room, but the glass door was closed. Ted sat on the floor beside the dog in front of the door. He put an arm around the animal's neck and, talking softly, calmed him down. With his other hand he tackled the complicated job of extracting the animal's fur from the engine's clockwork.

We heard the anti-aircraft guns booming in the distance. "Is that Granddad pounding on the table for more food?" murmured Ted. We laughed silently.

Winston panicked and tensed his body at the sound. I comforted him more. We spoke in whispers because we knew that, on the other side of the door, they were conducting their séance. Uncle Ted's ear pressed hard against the keyhole. I strained to look through the frosted glass panels.

My family and their friends were seated around a table. In an armchair at one end sat Mrs. Grimes, who breathed deeply. Her face, with the red light shining directly on it, was contorted. Irregularities in the door's glass gave everyone a distorted shape, like in the hall of magic mirrors.

"We have a contact," Mrs. Grimes gasped. "Can I bring him down?"

"Who," asked Grandmother?

"He says he will tell you when he gets down. He's strong now."

"Let him down," chipped in Mother. "Perhaps we knew him once."

Mrs. Grimes writhed in her armchair. "Oh! It's a transformation." Chest puffed out, prominent chin extended forward, Mrs. Grimes breathing deepened. She gurgled.

"I am here to pass on important news," she squawked.

"Who are you and for whom is the news?" Grandmother spoke clearly and firmly. Lilly giggled nervously from the back of the room.

The locomotive buzzed into life for a moment, winding more fur into its mechanism. Winston whimpered and jerked forward but Uncle Ted, arm around the dog's neck, restrained him. Ted's other hand laboured on to untangle the clockwork locomotive. I continued my efforts to calm the dog by stroking his head.

I pressed my face onto the pane of frosted glass to see more. Mrs. Grimes's expression was twisted, her cheeks bulged.

Mrs. Grimes, in her new voice, rasped, "Why don't you leave me alone and bugger off?"

"Oh!" exclaimed Grandmother.

"What do you want, you old lard pot?"

"Who are you?" repeated Grandmother.

"Sometimes I am a creature of the night, sometimes I am he who comes for you. I can be many things! Would you like me to be your friend?"

"Well, yes, I suppose we would."

"Then prove it," the voice squawked. Sweat poured down the sides of Mrs. Grimes' face. "We can prove our friendship through action," squawked Mrs. Grimes. Grandmother looked concerned.

Mrs. Grimes lurched forward in her chair, her transformation now a frightening caricature, her contorted voice rasped, "Action. Action! I'll give you action." Eyes wide, Mrs. Grimes stared at the door. Could she see my face pressed against the frosted glass panels?

"End it now, please. He's up to no good." Mother's voice faded into a whisper.

"Ooh! I want to spend a penny," added Lilly.

"Gertie, I think we should stop this now. Come out of the trance," urged Grandmother. Once again the clockwork whirled, pulling in more fur. Winston growled, fear changed to anger, anger turned to action.

Winston's limbs stiffened, then silently, with a thump, he lunged forward, breaking from Ted's grasp, paws scratching on the door. Lilly screamed, "See, oh Gawd, an 'orrible face in the door!" Everyone turned to look. Did she mean me?

The red light crashed to the floor, making the room darker. It flickered on and off, casting eerie shadows from its new angle.

In the semi-darkness, Winston, breaking away from Uncle Ted, forced the door open; his long, sleek, black form, a fast moving blur, streaked into the dining room and headed for Mrs. Grimes.

The clockwork engine's horn activated for the first time, emitting sharp, eerie hoots. Winston leaped onto Mrs. Grimes and licked her face. In panic, she snapped out of her trance crying, "Aaah! Oh my Lord! Bealzebub's among us! He has materialized!" Shrieks and yells filled the darkness, chairs tipped, and crockery crashed.

My last view of these events was of Grandfather, arms extended, face illuminated by a dull red flickering glow, calling out, "Jesus Christ. Why? Why me, Lord? What have I done to offend you?" He looked upwards. "Jesus, what did I do to deserve this?" The palms of his hands were open and facing the heavens. Were they waiting for nails to be hammered through? Was he waiting for the crucifixion?

Uncle Ted and I fled via the stairs to the box room, hoping to avoid detection.

"Quick, let's play with the train set and pretend that we know nothing." A great idea, but we lacked one important item: the engine.

Poor Uncle Ted. He was in serious trouble. Later, the whole household heard Grandfather, who refused to listen to Ted's explanation of what happened, loudly lecture him on the honourable treatment of household guests.

~~~***~~~

Tim's Dinner

Phil Yeats

Many years ago, a new family with two young children and two cats moved in next to us. Tim, the older of the cats, was a large ginger tom with a confident air, tattered ears, and other battle scars that showed he was a force to reckon with. He quickly asserted ownership of our house and yard, and began periodic visits of inspection. He would sit outside the patio door leading from our kitchen to the back deck, staring into the house. If we didn't open the door quickly enough, he would scratch on the glass to get our attention. After a greeting that seemed more like a scolding if we didn't let him in promptly, he would do his inspection before leaping onto one of our living room chairs for an afternoon nap. Around dinnertime, he would sit meowing by one of the doors until someone let him out.

These visits occurred two or three times a week for almost five years, from the time he arrived in the neighbourhood until shortly before he died at the ripe old age of 18.

One day, about six months before he died, Tim came as usual for a visit. Climbing the stairs onto the back deck had become difficult for him, and his inspections were now curtailed. He no longer went to check out the basement, and only wandered through two or three of the main floor rooms before settling down in his favourite chair. Climbing onto the chair, only 15 inches above the carpet, had become a struggle for the arthritic old cat.

On this particular day, he slept in his chair for several hours. None of us gave him any thought as we started preparations for dinner.

"How about the Spanish noodle skillet dinner from the Mennonite cookbook?" Linda suggested to our daughter and me from the living room doorway. Amelia had her head buried in a text book and didn't respond.

"Fine with me," I replied. "What do you need me to do?"

"Cut up the onion and green pepper, and brown the hamburger after I get the bacon cooked, please."

Twenty minutes later three crisp pieces of bacon were set aside on a paper towel, the hamburger was browned, and the cut up vegetables, as well as the spices and a can of stewed tomatoes, were all added to the fry pan. We both left the room while the concoction simmered.

"Tim, you monster!" Linda yelled from the kitchen, just minutes after I left. "Get down off that counter immediately!"

I heard the patio door slide shut as I hurried into the kitchen. Linda was bent over laughing, and pointing at Tim outside the door. He had a stunned look on his face and a piece of bacon protruding from his mouth. The wily old warrior had taken advantage of our absence, and proved he still had some life in his old legs.

"Man, was he up on the counter?" I exclaimed.

"Yes. He stole a piece of bacon, and was calmly chomping it up as if there was nothing wrong."

"Wow, a few hours ago he could barely climb up on one of the living room chairs and now he has the strength to leap three feet onto the counter."

"I'm not the least bit surprised," Amelia said from the doorway. "If I was a cat, I'd jump twice that high for some bacon. What are we going to do with the other two pieces?"

"No way I'm eating them after Tim's been sniffing around," Linda replied.

"That's what I thought you'd say," Amelia said, biting into a rasher and offering the other to me.

"Groossss!" Linda dragged out the word as she headed to the fridge for more bacon.

From that day onward, we called Spanish noodle skillet, "Tim's dinner".

***

Many years have passed and Tim is long gone. Amelia has a family of her own living in another city, but Linda and I have remained in our family home. Every month or so we have Tim's dinner for our evening meal, and whenever we do, I swear I hear a little scratching noise at the patio door in the kitchen. When I go outside to see if a tree branch is rubbing against the door or the adjacent window, there's nothing to be seen. But once the door is open, I always have the impression that something passes me as I go out.

I know it makes no sense, and Tim's ghost cannot have entered, but I always break one or two pieces off the rashers of cooked bacon waiting on the paper towel, and place them aside for Tim to find. Later, when it is time to crumble the bacon and return it to the fry pan, those pieces have always disappeared.

"Did you eat the bits I left for Tim?" I invariably ask Linda.

She always replies, "Of course not. You and Amelia are the only ones crude enough to eat bacon a cat's been sniffing."

But they're never there. I know I haven't eaten them and Amelia lives 4,000 miles away, so where have they gone?

~~~***~~~

Room 428

Catherine A. MacKenzie

Ocean's End Hotel, Cape Chignecto, Nova Scotia

1890

Alice gazed out the window, watching the distant fog slowly advancing over the water toward the hotel. Smudges and water stains distorted the glorious view of the Atlantic Ocean and added to her foreboding.

Mason, her husband's son, was riding, which he did every day. He'd come into view soon; she could count on him like clockwork. Him and his horse, Chamois. She thought Chamois a silly name for a horse.

The previous year when he'd purchased the mare, he had said it was the perfect name for her. "Just feel her. She's so soft, like a baby's breath, gentle, beautiful...."

She saw something akin to lust in his eyes, and jealousy spread through her. "It'll turn on you someday," Alice said. She— Alice—should have been enough for him. His eyes should have been on her, not on some dratted animal.

She sighed, her heavy breath making a perfect circle on the glass.

Eventually, Alice gave up waiting, donned her husband's hat and coat, and ventured to the balcony where she sat on a weathered chair. She pulled a cigar from the pocket of Freeman's trench coat and took her first drag of the day.

She'd been dying for that moment. While Alice took another puff, and another, and another, she watched for Mason.

***

Mason struggled with the reins. Chamois was acting ornery. Mason tried to pull her in, but the animal was determined to have its own way.

"Whoa, girl. Calm down. Steady, steady." Mason's words were in vain, and Chamois veered away from the well-trampled path and toward the cliff's edge, east of Ocean's End Hotel.

Chamois galloped closer and closer to the cliff. The waves below whipped against the boulders, the sound not unlike hundreds of frenzied fathers attacking screaming children with endless belt lashes. Mason bit his lower lip, tasting blood mixed with the salty mist. Menacing clouds scudded above him as if racing away from danger. Several colossal crows circled and chanted their incessant, piercing *caw caw caw!*

When he passed the hotel, Mason glimpsed a figure on the balcony. Thick smoke curled above the individual, who exhaled perfect curlicues that soon disappeared.

"Whoa, girl," he shouted again. "Stop!"

The person, who was too small to be Mason's father, stood and looked his way. There was a familiarity about the way the stranger rose from the chair, but Mason couldn't recognize him, not with a hat covering his head and a coat's collar reaching his chin. Why was the small man bundled as if for a blizzard when the early evening, though damp, was mild?

Mason yanked on the reins again. The edge, where the cliff dropped 500 feet to a jumble of rocks and boulders, neared. Surely Chamois would not gallop any closer?

The mare's pace slackened. "Good, girl," Mason mumbled. His words were barely out before the animal picked up speed and galloped toward the cliff's edge once again. Inches from land's end—so close he felt the earth separate and give way under the animal's hooves—Chamois came to a full stop and abruptly turned sideways. In one slick motion, the horse hurled Mason toward the horizon.

July 1927

Reginald glimpsed Elizabeth, his wife, approaching. He grasped her elbow when she reached him. "Elizabeth, love, I want you to meet an old friend. This is Duncan Dunn. We studied at Dalhousie together. We've been talking about old times."

Elizabeth extended her hand and smiled. "Nice to meet you, Duncan."

"My pleasure."

"Duncan graduated a year ahead of me. What year was that? 1913? Or was that my year? Age is taking its toll." Reginald chuckled as he glanced at his old friend.

"Old age? You're younger than me, Reginald. What are you, 38?"

Elizabeth laughed. "I think we're all in the same boat. I'm forgetting everything nowadays as well, and I'm younger than both of you. How long are you here, Duncan?"

"Just overnight. Catching a ride to Amherst in the morning, then the train to Halifax."

Reginald faced his wife and interjected, "I told Duncan how you and I are here for a short vacation."

"Yes, Reg is Truro's sheriff. Did he tell you that? He's been so busy." Without waiting for an answer, she continued. "This is the perfect place for a rest. So secluded and quiet. And the weather is beautiful this time of year. We're going to take a walk through the woods tomorrow morning, if the bugs aren't too bad. Right, Reggie?"

"Yes, dear, whatever you want."

Duncan glanced at his watch. "Sorry, but I must run. Might catch you in the morning before I head out. If I don't, have a pleasant time and a safe trip home."

"Safe travels to you, too," Reginald said.

Elizabeth gazed at Duncan and held out her hand once more. "Nice to have met you, Duncan. Perhaps we'll meet again sometime."

Duncan accepted her hand and held it to his lips a second longer than necessary.

Reginald watched his friend leave. "Haven't seen him since he graduated. Nice to have run into him. Hasn't changed much. He always was a wild one."

"Wild?"

"Liked the women, if you know what I mean." Reginald snickered.

"I see." Elizabeth paused. "Perhaps I'll go to my room and rest up. Finish my book, maybe, if you're going to play poker."

"I'd like to, if you don't mind. The game starts at ten. I'll go to the bar first."

"Stay as long as you like. I'll be fine."

"Should be over by midnight." Reginald kissed his wife on the cheek before heading to the bar.

* * *

Reginald gulped the last of his rum. He glanced at the clock hanging over the bar, surprised it was only 9:45 p.m. He'd already decided to pass on the poker game. For some reason, he wasn't in the mood. Perhaps he'd had too much to drink.

"I'm going to head in," he told the bartender. "Put the tab on room 428, will ya?"

Donning his hat, he headed to the staircase. At the top of the stairs, he stopped to catch his breath and then turned right toward his room. He retrieved the brass key from his pocket and, not wanting to wake his wife, stealthily inserted it into the door.

At first, he didn't realize anything was amiss. The moon's rays shone into the room, enough illumination for him to make his way to the bathroom, yet something made him hesitate. There appeared to be more than one person in the bed.

When his suspicion registered, he froze. *What the hell!*

Reginald coughed, a nervous reaction. Whatever hid beneath the blankets stirred.

Two figures, once shrouded by linens and darkness, bolted upright. The bedclothes concealed the lower halves of their bodies, but the beam of moonlight trapped the couple in its glow. The light framed the two lovers as though they were meant to be together, like a hurriedly snapped photograph of a recently married couple. Except they weren't a married couple. And they didn't sport happy faces. One was Reginald's dearly beloved Elizabeth. It took a few long seconds before he recognized his college buddy, Duncan.

Tongue-tied, Reginald stared. The couple had apparently lost their voices, as well.

Reginald coughed again, on purpose, which injected life, albeit sluggish movement, into the shadowed room. Before Elizabeth or Duncan reacted, Reginald reached inside his jacket and withdrew his gun.

He pulled the trigger. The flashes produced eerie luminescence when he fired two precise shots before the unsuspecting couple were able to jump from the bed or regain their voices. Tears formed in his eyes as the force threw the individuals—first Duncan and then Elizabeth—backward on the bed where they lay as if never disturbed.

Reginald spewed a thick wad of phlegm to the floor before tossing the Smith & Wesson onto the bed. He visualized the blood of the two lovers mingling as the thick fluid seeped into the mattress. The raw acridness wafted toward him though the smell was probably in his mind. He knew from his investigations into dozens of homicides that the pungent, metallic odour wouldn't fill his nostrils that fast unless he stood in a slaughterhouse.

He clutched his unbuttoned coat around him before unlatching the balcony door and stepping outside. The full moon hung low in the sky, and to Reginald's numb mind, it seemed ready to swing down and snuff him out. Stars twinkled mockingly in the sky, their sharp edges piercing his skin and gouging his heart. He leaned against the balcony and, despite the darkness, stared far ahead to where he knew the Atlantic Ocean met the horizon. Below him, the ocean smashed its furious fists against the boulders. To his left, in the distance, Cape d'Or Lighthouse radiated.

As if possessed, he hoisted himself to the balcony railing, throwing first one leg and then the other over the wide strip of wood. With one final look into the room where his once-beloved wife lay, he let himself topple to the rocks below.

September 1927

"Room 428. Up the staircase. Fourth floor and to your right," Ned said as he handed the keys to Mr. and Mrs. Doucette. "It's a nice room overlooking the ocean, with a balcony. Just remodelled. Checkout is 11 a.m."

Marcus smiled at his bride. Gail grinned in return when he grazed her arm, causing goose bumps. "Let's go."

When Marcus reached for the suitcases, the porter appeared by his side. "Allow me, sir."

Once in the room, Marcus tipped the porter and closed the door. He smothered his new wife to his chest and gave her a passionate kiss. "It's late, honey, should we get to bed?"

"You tired?" Gail winked.

"It *is* our honeymoon."

Gail laughed. "Yes, it is. And don't you ever forget our date of September 12, 1927. I don't want a husband who forgets his anniversary." She turned toward the bed and noticed the framed picture hanging on the wall. "What an odd picture," she said. "Who'd want a picture of an ugly horse like that on the wall, especially in a hotel room?"

"Never you mind that," Marcus said as he moved toward his wife.

An hour later, the two dreamt of their happy future until Gail, who faced the window, stirred when the moonlight swept into the room. She blinked at the blinding glare, wishing she'd pulled the drapes across the balcony door.

"Marcus," she whispered. "You awake?"

Not receiving an answer, she rolled over and scooted toward her husband. Just before she spooned into him, intending to lay her arm across his chest, a chilling dampness swept over her. He felt cold. And clammy. Usually Marcus was as hot as a furnace blasting forth on a frigid winter's day. Her arm, having first touched something solid, suddenly slipped into nothingness. Chills flickered up and down her skin as if a foreign object slithered through her body.

"Marcus!" Gail screeched before bounding to the floor. "Ahhhhhck!"

When two shadowy figures arose in the bed, a gunshot echoed in the sudden darkness. She covered her ears and screamed again. "Marcus!"

Marcus jumped from the bed. "Gail, honey, what is it? What's the matter? Calm down."

Gail's hands flew to her mouth. The bodies in the bed rose to lengthen into vaporous, wriggling serpents and slithered across the wall. As if rooted to the floor, she couldn't budge. She wanted to move. It was only a few feet to the door—only a few feet to escape from the spectres. They were after her—those flat, eel-like creatures.

Marcus grabbed her, crushing her tight to his chest. Sobbing, she clung to him and pressed her face against him. Why weren't they racing to the door? She gathered the courage and looked up at his face. "We have to go. We have to get out of here." She squirmed, but he held her tighter. Nervously, she glanced around the room.

"Shhh, shhh. You must've had a bad dream. It's okay now. "Shhh." Marcus patted her head to calm her down.

"No, it's real...they were there—bodies in the bed...dead bodies...holding onto one another...wouldn't let me go...thought it was you." She pointed at the bed, trying to catch her breath in between her rushed words.

Marcus glanced at the bedclothes askew on the floor. "Honey, there's no one there. Wait, let me get the light. See, just you and me."

"No, Marcus, there were two people in that bed with us. Two dead people!" she shrieked, clinging to him again. "You must have seen them; you had to have seen them! And one I touched. It was horrible, so disgusting!"

"Shhh, honey, shhh. Let's get back to bed. It's late."

"No. No. I absolutely...no, I won't sleep in this room. There's something here. I can feel it. A presence. An eerie presence. Spying on us. I can smell the blood. Can't you smell it?"

"No, Gail, I can't. Calm down."

"I know what I saw. I know what I heard. I'm out of here, with or without you." Gail wrestled out of his arms and, naked, headed to the door.

"Okay, okay. I'll go to the front desk and see if there's another available room." Marcus pulled on his pants. "Wait here. I'll go see."

"Oh, no you're not. No way. I'm coming with you. You're not leaving me alone in here." Suddenly realizing her nakedness, she grabbed her robe.

They made their way to the lobby. After ringing the desk bell several times, Ned emerged from a door behind the desk. He rubbed his bleary eyes and suppressed a yawn.

"There are ghosts. I saw them." Gail blubbered. Her arms flailed. Marcus half-heartedly corroborated his wife's statements.

Ned glanced from Gail to Marcus. "Ah, yes. Room 428." After a pause while he searched for words, he continued. "That's our best room. There's no such thing as ghosts. Not in this hotel. You are the first guests in that room since it was remodelled."

Gail, despite her frenzy, glimpsed the recognition that washed over Ned's face. "You know something, don't you? I don't care a fig what you say. There's something about that room, isn't there?"

Ned glanced away.

"Gail, hush." Marcus put his arm around his wife.

"He knows something. Something about that room. It's haunted, isn't it?" Gail glared at Ned. "I want another room. I'd leave this hotel for good, but it's too late to go anywhere else."

"No, ma'am, there are no ghosts. The hotel—the room—isn't haunted. I know no such thing." Ned leafed through his book, turned around, and pulled a key from the slot. "Here, room 202. I'm sorry for your bad experience. This room is on the house. I'll refund your money in the morning. Let me help move your bags."

"That's quite okay," Marcus said. "We can handle it. Come on, Gail, let's get moved so we can get back to sleep. Morning will be here before we know it."

"I'll wait in the new room while you get our stuff."

"If you like, you can leave your things there till morning," Ned suggested.

"No." Gail shot more daggers at Ned. "I want our stuff out of there now. You hear me, Marcus? Now!"

Marcus and Gail headed to the stairs. Gail, out of breath when they reached the second floor, said, "There's something fishy. He knows something's wrong. Why else would he give us a free room?"

"Oh, Gail, he just wants to keep his guests happy."

Marcus unlocked the door to room 202. "Wait here. I'll be back in a few minutes with our belongings."

1938

Sally, the chambermaid, hesitated before room 428. She *pooh-poohed* the tales about the hotel and room 428 in particular. A murder and suicide about 10 years previously was common knowledge around the area. There was nothing odd about it, just an explicable happenstance sparked by jealousy, rage, and despair. The weirdest and scariest stories were the ones about guests who woke up in bed to find bodies beside them, except they weren't real, of course. They must have been ghosts, for what else could they be? And then there were bodies that fell from the balcony and disappeared. Not to mention other mysterious tales generated by the rumour mill and gossip gone amuck.

There were few jobs in Cape Chignecto for a 56-year-old woman, and Sally was elated when hired as one of three chambermaids at Ocean End's Hotel. A few ghosts wouldn't stop her.

She tiptoed over the threshold. Her eyes darted about the room. "Get hold of yourself," she mumbled. "It's just another room to be cleaned for the next guests."

Sally stripped the bed and gathered the soiled towels. She scrubbed the tub and sink and placed clean, folded towels on the rack. To others, those were mundane chores, but Sally took pride in her work. If she did a job, it was going to be done right, whatever task it might be.

Later that day, Harry, the manager, accosted Sally in the laundry room. "Sally, did you finish with room 428?"

"Yes, sir."

His eyes narrowed and his tone of voice held rebuke. "I sent a guest up there earlier. He came back in a huff, said it was a mess."

"It was spotless when I left it, sir. What's the problem?"

"It's a mess, I told you. I just went up there myself. Get back in there and clean it up."

Sally glared at her boss. "But it was neat as a pin when I left." She couldn't help but notice Harry's face suddenly pale, just before he turned away.

"Get it straightened up. Now!"

Sally climbed the staircase, shaking her head and muttering. She didn't know what was happening, but she didn't like being accused of not doing her job. By the time she reached the fourth floor, she gasped for breath and rested for a few seconds. She hesitated again before the locked door to room 428. The last thing she wanted to do was open the door, but she'd lose her job if she didn't.

She fiddled with the key before the door opened. She stared in disbelief when she saw the disarray. It would take her hours to put it back to order. What on earth had happened?

Dirt had been trampled on the carpet, leaving large footprints. Empty dresser drawers lay toppled in a heap. Pillows had been ripped apart, and a few straggled feathers floated in the breeze from the open balcony door. Dirty towels and linens lay strewn about the room. She gritted her teeth and sighed. "This is what I've heard before. The ghosts in the beds. The unexplained disorder.

Harry knows this mess isn't normal. It's the apparitions that have come. Yes, siree, them ghosts have come."

Then her practical side took over. "I'll show them," she muttered. "This room will be back to normal in no time."

1950

Clyde MacDonald stared at the deceptively calm water. The ocean fascinated him—how it spewed its guts one day and rolled in as soft as a baby's breath the next. Ocean's End Hotel was similar, its usual serenity disturbed by periodic machinations of strange apparitions that haunted the place.

Business had been slow for years, and word of sightings and unnatural happenings hadn't helped. Fewer and fewer people wanted to stay at Ocean's End Hotel. Over the years, he'd lost workers, as well as guests. Once the number of guests slackened off, it was necessary to fire staff. He couldn't afford to pay the help when money wasn't coming in. Even his trusty manager, Simon, left.

Cape Chignecto was situated about half-way between Eatonville and Advocate Harbour, both 20 kilometres away. Why his ancestors had built such an establishment at that locale never ceased to puzzle him, though the nearby residents must have been elated. The MacDonalds originally settled in Eatonville, established by the Eaton family in 1864, and several years later Freeman MacDonald built Ocean's End Hotel high up on Cape Chignecto. Eatonville's population at its peak, when his grandparents resided there, would have been about 350 souls, but the village had been almost abandoned by the 1930s, with the last year-round resident leaving in 1943. Advocate Harbour still thrived—somewhat—and boasted residents who fished for a living. Those folks, however, didn't frequent his hotel.

Why had he remained? Why had he listened to his father and taken over the place? Running a hotel had never been an aspiration. Still, he tried to make a go of it, marketing the area as a tourist attraction to the bigger cities like Halifax, approximately 250 kilometres away. City folk liked to get away from hustle and bustle, and nothing existed on Cape Chignecto except the hotel as a final destination—nothing but the vast wilderness and the endless horizon, a prime location for relaxation.

Stories of shipwrecks lured a few people, as did lurid renditions of ever-present ghost stories. The excitement of exploring caves and tunnels at the base of the cliff that might contain the remains of missing guests also attracted some visitors. He constantly admonished the managers to warn those searching for undiscovered caves and exploring mysterious tunnels to be back on high ground before the tide turned, for once the water came in, there would be no escape. He also advised his employees to point out the dangers of powerful currents that could suck individuals into whirlpools or carry them out to sea.

Perhaps the dangers—real and imagined—were just too much for anyone to endure.

Clyde had to accept reality; he couldn't keep the hotel running any longer. The century-old wooden edifice's time had expired.

A tingling sensation coursed through him. He looked up to the rolling clouds, certain one stopped to hover over him. Campbell MacDonald, his grandfather, surely peered down on him. The old man, despite being deceased for several decades, wouldn't be happy with the course the hotel had taken. Clyde had spent happy summers with his grandparents at the hotel, never noticing anything out of the ordinary while he stayed there.

Clyde's parents, not wanting to live in the boonies nor run a hotel, hired managers while they remained in Halifax. Upon his graduation from university, Clyde's father convinced him to take over the hotel. Clyde didn't want to live at the hotel, so he continued his parents' practice of hiring managers to run the place. Every few weeks he travelled from Halifax to Cape Chignecto to ensure the hotel ran properly and kept in frequent contact by telephone, but his efforts were in vain. The business was losing money, and he couldn't afford to keep subsidizing it.

He had to close the hotel. For good. It was time.

An unknown force propelled him to take the key for room 428 and head up the stairs. He opened the door, immediately seeing the framed painting of the horse. He hadn't taken much notice of it previously, but that day it sneered at him. The mouth came alive, its lips peeled away to reveal blood-red gums and huge, yellowed teeth. Clyde had to rub his eyes several times to rid himself of the image that flared before him. Since when had it hung in the bedroom? It had been displayed in the lobby when his grandfather was alive. When he looked again, the picture was back to normal.

Then, Clyde watched in horror as one by one empty drawers ejected from the dresser and toppled to the floor. The bed rose, hoisted evenly by the four bedposts. The flowered comforter drifted up and off the bed. The pillows floated alongside the comforter before flying across the room toward him.

Although the sun streamed through the balcony door, the room darkened. Shadows seeped from under the floorboards, from inside the closet, from behind the mirror. A sudden flash of light highlighted dark shadows rising to the ceiling. Once there, the shapes morphed into a white cloud. A foggy substance hovered for a few seconds before disappearing, as if the apparition had fragmented into the air and its particles absorbed into nothingness. Clyde shivered and held his breath.

A breeze swirled around him, and he recoiled at the malodorous odour—warm and sickly-sweet, foul like rotten horse breath—before the speed of the air intensified and spun him around. He opened his mouth to scream and then just as quickly closed it. The wind became stronger, and he was afraid to breathe, scared he might inhale too much too fast. He let himself go limp, allowed his body to ascend to the ceiling in the hope the episode would soon be over.

He heard the silence before realizing he'd been released from what possessed him. Oddly exhilarated, he felt he had slept for two solid days. In the far distance a man and a woman screamed. A gunshot followed. The last sound he heard was a horse's neigh. He had never liked animals, had never been around them much. Why was that the last sound he heard?

Today

Frank gazes at several patches of crumbling concrete—all that remains of Ocean's End Hotel. The hotel had been in the MacDonald family from its construction in 1869 until the 1950s. At one time, he thought, it must have been a bustling, thriving establishment. After its collapse and demolition, the province of Nova Scotia turned the land into a provincial park.

Although the hotel was abandoned when Frank first saw it as a child, he remembers the building standing like an unconquerable fortress. Although uncertain why, the building scared him. Frank thinks back to his teenage years and the papers he and his father found when they were walking on the fourth floor. Frank tripped over a protruding floorboard. When his father bent down to help him up, his father mumbled several incoherent words before he yanked out the rotten board. The older man pulled out a batch of weathered papers, glanced at them, and then stuck them under his arm. When Frank inquired as to the discovery, his father clammed up saying they were some old bills.

Because of his father's changed and secretive attitude, Frank knew otherwise. When his parents left for the store, Frank withdrew the papers from the desk where he had seen his father stash them. Frank's first thought was that they were pages from a diary, obviously important ones since they'd been stored there for a reason. But why? And who had put them there?

Frank scanned the papers, not understanding much of what was written, not at the time, but years later when he overheard his father and grandfather rehashing the goings on in the hotel, the words held more meaning. That was when he figured Alice, the wife of Freeman MacDonald, had written them, since they appeared to be written by a woman pining for someone other than her husband. Over the years, he had heard of Alice and how the family in later generations blamed every catastrophe befalling Ocean's End Hotel on her.

The several pages from Alice's diary, the edges of the paper lightly charred, were stuffed between other sheets, written by another individual, more or less updating happenings later—how Alice had disappeared leaving her diary behind in the lit fireplace. Whoever wrote the other pages had entered the room, found the dying fire and, puzzled as to why and who had started a fire on a hot summer's day, discovered the slightly charred book.

Alice's words spoke of her untold grief after her stepson, Mason, with whom she had carried on an inappropriate relationship, had died. Later, she became more unhinged when Duncan, her biological son from a previous marriage, had been killed. Sightings of a woman—Alice—lingering about the hotel were rampant in future years.

Frank heard other explanations of ghostly tales. One was that Reginald, hoping he could change the past, continually returned to room 428 to re-enact the night he had discovered his unfaithful wife.

Unable to bring her back, he caused mayhem in the room. Another stated the spectral bodies occasionally found in bed with guests were the ghosts of Duncan and Elizabeth. Yet another snippet offered the opinion that because Alice's and Mason's souls could not rest, they continually searched for a bed where they could sleep peacefully. They always ended up in room 428 because Alice wanted to be close to where Duncan died.

None of the yellowed papers dealt with Clyde's generation. Clyde, the great-grandfather Frank never met, vanished just before he was to close the hotel for good in 1950. The mystery of Clyde's disappearance had never been solved.

"Who knows for certain what the truth is. If there is any truth at all." Frank sighs for all that has been lost—the hotel, his ancestors, but mainly the truth.

He stares into the distance. The well-known Bay of Fundy fog will soon settle and camouflage everything in sight. Mist has already dampened Frank's face. He rolls his tongue across his salted lips. Several seagulls flap over the vast ocean, their squawking the only sound marring the calm of the wilderness. The birds' black markings blend in with the darkening sky. Perhaps a storm is brewing.

Frank shrugs and heads back to his car. He stops at the sound of a harsh wail, reminding him of a horse's whinny. But where would a horse be in that wilderness? Did he imagine the sound of a horse, since he just rehashed past events? The noise brings back remembrances of a picture of a horse from his childhood. He doesn't remember seeing it in the hotel when he last traipsed the building when he was a teenager, not that he was actively searching for it. The painting was the ugliest picture of a horse he'd ever seen. And who would ever paint a portrait of a horse?

He looks back. More inquisitive gulls appear from nowhere. Their grace in flight captivates him as their large wings whip through the air. While Frank watches, the descending fog shrouds the cliff's edge. Is that a puff of smoke circling above the edge of the cliff? A small animal scurries and disappears into the bush. The seagulls fade into the murkiness. The haze spreads toward him like smoke from an untamed wildfire.

~~~***~~~

The Ghosts' Night Out, or Bats in the Belfry

Maida Follini

"The thing I hate about being dead," said Frank, "is not being able to speak to my grandson."

"If I spoke to my granddaughter, I'd scare her out of her wits," William replied, from his plot next to Frank's in the Union Church Cemetery. William and Frank had been neighbours in life for over 20 years, William's white clapboard Colonial next to Frank's brick Federal home on Elm Street in the little town of Sparrow Falls, Eden County, Nova Scotia. Now they had neighbouring plots in the churchyard, although Frank had occupied his plot several years before William moved into his.

Frank had a yard-high pink granite gravestone at the head of his plot, with "In Loving Memory" over his name, "Francis Bigelow Cranston". Below was the name of his wife, "Amelia" with her date of birth and a blank space left for her death date. Amelia had not yet joined him. She was in a retirement home at the edge of town. William, on the other hand, had a simple marble marker, provided by the government, as he was a veteran. On it was his name, "William Barrington Scott", his rank in the Navy, "Seaman First Class", birth and death dates, and place of service, "Korea". William's wife, Janet, had gone to live with their son in Florida. But she sent flowers every year for William's grave.

"I wouldn't want to scare little Jack," Frank went on. "I'd speak to him softly. I'd give him advice about playing marbles, and coach him when he had a test in school."

"I don't think I'd scare my grandson, Marty," said William. "He's a skeptical teenager. If he saw me, he'd just say, 'I don't believe in ghosts. You're just a hologram!'"

"Well, he couldn't see you, any more than Jackie can hear me," said Frank. "If only we could make them hear! It's such a hindrance not to have any *power!* No *substance!* Just floating ectoplasm, wafting around, slipping through doors like light through a window, and not being able to leave our mark anywhere!"

"We can hear each other, but they can't." William spoke of the living people they watched and visited whenever they left the retirement of their grave plots. "And we can't even touch them! The other night I wanted to push my son-in-law out of the Lodge meeting where they were all wasting time arguing about whether to paint the Lodge building white or green!"

Frank shook his airy head in disgust. "Why don't they live a little, instead of argel-bargeling? We're just useless vapours. Floating around, watching them make mistakes." At his hardware store, Frank had been used to handing out advice and fixing everyone's problems.

"If only we could find a way to influence them!" William had been the editor of the town paper, where he had considered it his duty to write influential editorials.

The sun had set, darkness had fallen. William began edging his way out of his narrow grave. "Coming?" he enquired.

"Just as soon as I can get around this humungous stone my lovely wife placed on top of me," Frank replied. "Not that I don't appreciate it. She meant it for the best, and I suppose it made her feel better."

"Oh, go on! You'd be insulted if you had a little flat plaque on the ground that no one could see, like old Crowley, there!" Crowley was their neighbour in the cemetery, as unpopular in death as in life.

Frank and William floated up from the ends of their plots, resting a minute on Frank's large headstone to check the weather. A calm night meant moving deliberately and slowly where they intended to go. Rain had a tendency to wash them to the ground, while wind—well, once Frank had been blown in a gale nearly to the next county and it had taken him three nights to get back.

Tonight there was only a moderate breeze, making the tree-branches tremble and the traffic-light in the centre of town sway on its cable. Helped by the breeze, the two ghosts were soon in the town square, pausing on the bell-tower of the town hall and surveying the scene. The town of Sparrow Falls was built along a river where a disused mill recalled a previous busy age. In the centre of town, a few stores, the library and a few churches clustered around the Common. From here, some business blocks spread along Main Street, and residential streets ran off on each side. Among the houses with green lawns and shrubbery in front, vegetable gardens and tool sheds in back, were the former homes of Frank Cranston and William Scott—now the homes of their grown children.

Frank swooped down to a lighted window of his son's house. "Working late on bills, looks like." Frank watched as his son suddenly threw down an envelope on a pile of a dozen others, pushed back his chair, and groaned. The room door opened and his wife appeared.

"Don't do any more tonight, honey. It's too late." The room darkened as they exited, footsteps on the stairs were heard, and soon a light appeared on the second floor.

William had been watching as his daughter put her little girl to bed. Little Kirstey's room was filled with stuffed animals, her collection of china horses, and her favourite books. Her mother tucked her in, and turned out the light, while her husband called to their teenage son, Marty. "Turn out the lights downstairs, school tomorrow. Time to turn in."

"Ha!" William said. "They think Kirstey's in bed, but she's gotten up and is looking out the window at the moon. And Marty has gone out to the shed. What's he doing out there?"

Marty had gone out with his flashlight and was poking around the dark corners of the shed.

Frank called. "Come on. I want to see who's on the night train from Truro. Last week a whole bunch of theatre people came in for a performance at the Legion Hall."

The two friends drifted off. But when the night train pulled in to the tiny carpenter's gothic station and creaked to a stop, the only passengers who got off were a group of college students returning from their evening courses at the Community College. With quite a bit of noise they set off in various directions, calling: "Good night!" "See you tomorrow!" "See you on Facebook!" "Meet you at the Caff!" "I'm going to skip tomorrow, send me a tweet!"

Frank and William, continuing their circle of the town, found it no more interesting. The pool hall showed two die-hards competing for a five-dollar bet. At the police station, Officer McQuestor sat at the wheel of an idling police car until his buddy

Constable Shivers came down the steps and jumped into the passenger seat. The car sped away.

"Off they go. Should we take after it?" Frank suggested.

"Probably just a barking dog or a treed cat," William replied. "Nothing interesting ever happens in this town."

As they caught the breeze bearing them back towards their old neighbourhood, Frank suddenly said, "Do you smell something?"

"Smoke!" William could see a stream of smoke coming from the woodshed by his daughter's house. "Oh, lord! It's a fire!"

Both of them could see flames now, lapping out from inside the shed, sending spears through the gaps in the wooden sides.

"It'll catch the houses! We have to do something!" Frank called in alarm. Even as they watched, the shed, whose side was practically touching William's daughter's house, sent sparks through its roof, sparks which landed on the home of Frank's son, just a few feet away.

"Fire! Fire!" both yelled. They did not have human voices, so of course no one could hear.

Frank slipped through the window to his son's bedroom and circled the sleepers. "I'd like to shake you!" he cried in frustration, as his son lay with his arm out, head back, snoring a little, his wife sound asleep, curled up with her head partly under the pillow.

William had slipped through the smoke and flame to his daughter's back doorstep. There was a full watering can by the step, but he had neither hands nor strength to lift it. "Oh, God, why am I so helpless?"

"We must do something!" Frank dropped beside William. "Come on! We must ring the bell and wake the town!"

"But how can we?" William groaned.

"We'll have to find a way. We must try!" Frank barrelled ahead, rising on the breeze as fast as he could to the top of the bell tower, two blocks away. William was beside him. The two ghosts slipped through the lattice where the great brass bell hung. It was heavy and immobile as the two franticly threw themselves against it.

"And I was 190 pounds when I was alive," Frank said, in despair. William whirled in anguish round and round the bell, leaving a stream of luminescence in his wake. Through the belfry slats he could see the flames reaching towards his daughter's home.

A rush, a flapping, a hundred squeaking cries. All at once, the two ghosts were enveloped in what seemed like a swarm of a hundred squealing, flying mice, their wings unfolding like small umbrellas, their eyes bright with alarm as they swirled around, trying to dodge the ghosts.

"Bats!"

"They see us!" said Frank.

"They hear us!" William realized. "They can hear things people can't hear!"

The bats circled away from the ghosts, hiding inside the bell, hanging upside down from the clapper. More and more of them swooped to get away from the ghosts until dozens—hundreds—covered the clapper. When the ghosts moved to one side of the bell-tower, the bats swerved to the opposite side of the clapper.

A soft clang rang out; the movement of the bats rocked the clapper.

"Move! Fly!" Frank and William rocketed around to keep the bats moving, to keep them seeking a safe place opposite the ghosts.

Clang! The clapper hit one side of the bell. *Clang!* With every clang the ghosts circled to the opposite side, making sure the bats kept moving back and forth.

Clang!

Windows were thrown up in the town below.

"What's the alarm? What's happening?"

The neighbours across the street saw the fire. "Call the fire department!" one shouted to his wife.

"Wake up the neighbours!" his wife called back.

Soon people were running up the street, shouting, pounding on house doors.

Clang! The ghosts kept the bats moving, flying, clinging inside the bell.

Clang! The bats kept the clapper moving.

The firehouse horn began sounding to call in the volunteers. The engine fired up and sirens howling, like a quarrelsome cat, roared up the street.

"Here's the hydrant!" a boy shouted. The hose men completed the hook-up while other firemen rushed inside the house, making sure everyone was out.

Frank's son stood in his pyjamas in the street, one arm around his wife, the other holding young Jack. "I don't know what happened," he kept saying. "What happened?"

William's daughter, her husband, and little Kirstey had stumbled down the stairs in their night things. Neighbours rushed to keep both families warm with blankets.

The fire chief told them, "It's mostly in the shed. Some of the siding on the houses caught fire, but we'll put it out without too much damage."

As the shock began to wear off, young Jackie and Kirstey climbed excitedly on the fire engine. Kirstey rang the engine's bell, and Jackie blew the horn repeatedly, a loud blasting blare, more like a freight train blast than an ordinary car horn.

Wrapped in blankets, the parents began to heave sighs of relief. The shed fire was easily put out, the nearby homes sprayed with water to prevent them from igniting. Steam rose from the remains of the shed.

"Marty, what are you doing?" William's daughter cried to her teenage son. Marty, upon discovering the fire was out, had sneaked back among the smoking wreckage of the shed.

"Nothing," he said. "I was just seeing that the fire was out."

The fire chief told his parents, "We'll stay until everything is completely out. Then tomorrow the inspector will come to see if he can find what caused the fire. Do any of you smoke?"

"Oh, no!" said William's daughter. "We're a smoke-free house. My husband gave it up years ago."

Marty, holding something under the blanket draped over his shoulders, moved off a little ways down the street, and dropped it into a neighbour's trash can.

William, who had hovered with Frank over the scene, once their service at the belfry was no longer needed, scrutinized his grandson. Now he knew what Marty had been doing out in the shed before going to bed. Sure enough, when William peered into the neighbour's trashcan, a pack had been discarded there, open, revealing a jumble of cigarettes falling out.

People were beginning to disperse. A couple of firemen and a police officer were assigned to stay on site and secure the scene. A reporter from William's old newspaper was interviewing Frank's family and the bystanders to find out what they had seen.

"But who rang the bell?" said Frank's son. "That's the person who should be interviewed. He gave the alarm and saved us all."

But no one seemed to know who gave the alarm. The policeman went up to the town hall to see if the alert citizen was still there.

"The door was locked from the outside," he reported. "Who had the key?" But no one except the janitor and the mayor had keys. They were among the crowd, and denied being the ones who rang the bell. Who could have gotten in?

"It must have been an angel," William's daughter said. And that's what was to appear in the paper the next day: "Mysterious Angel Rings Alarm Bell, Saves Families from Fire!"

"Well, I never thought I was an angel," said Frank.

"Me neither," replied William. "Do I look like an angel?" The two floated their way back to the graveyard, the excitement over, the crowd gone home.

As they slipped into their familiar graves, Frank said, "Well, at least one good thing about being dead is there's no one to holler at you for being out all night."

A grumbling voice came from the next grave plot. "Will you guys please shut up? I'm trying to get some rest."

"Old Crowley," said William.

"I take back that last remark," said Frank.

Silence settled over Union Church Cemetery.

~~~***~~~

The Once and Future Ghost
Janet McGinity

The clock struck 11 with a dull bong. Vera methodically wiped down the counter around the sink with a rag. With a weary sigh, she pushed hair off her face where it had come loose from her greying ponytail.

Vera rinsed the rag under hot water, wrung it out, and hung the damp cloth on the stove door handle. Then she opened the cabinet drawer to get a clean rag for tomorrow. The cloth resisted. It caught on a lump at the back. Vera tugged, and the rag finally came free. A small, heavy object snagged in a fold.

Curious, she pulled away the crumpled fabric, revealing a rose cameo. On the back of the stone was an open gold pin. Its sharp tip had stuck in the rag.

Vera held the cameo under the stove's fluorescent light to see it better. The profile was of a young woman, glassy white against the deep blush of the rose quartz background. Her hair was gathered back in a pompadour style, with tendrils escaping around the ear. Earrings glinted as small bumps against the relief.

"How strange," she mused. "It must have been at the back of the drawer. I wonder how long it's been there."

She opened the drawer all the way, finding a two-inch space where the back wall did not quite meet the bottom. Perhaps the cameo fell from the drawer above, which had the same space at the back. Vera occasionally found odd articles around the house, dropped or lost by the people who had lived there before she and her husband, Arnold, bought the old Bennett house 10 years ago. Last week, she found a Christmas card stuck between a bedroom wall and the baseboard. Faded copperplate writing wished, "Dear Maude, a happy and prosperous 1913."

Vera wondered about the woman who had worn the cameo. Might she be one of the Bennett girls? Vaguely, Vera remembered a photograph at the county museum of four laughing young women, arms entwined, carrying on in front of their home. Their long skirts, high-necked blouses, and pompadour hairstyles suggested a year around 1905. She thought one of the women might have worn a cameo on a ribbon around her neck.

"I must go to the museum and look at that photograph," she said to herself. "I'll do that tomorrow, if it's open." She took the cameo to the bedroom, and put it in a small cardboard jewellery box. The cameo seemed to pulsate against the white cotton wool lining. She ran her fingers lightly over the profile. It felt warm.

Vera frowned, closed the lid, and put the small box on the bedside table. She returned downstairs, checked that the front and back doors were locked, and turned out the lights like she did every night. The last thing she thought, before falling asleep, was that she must tell Arnold this Friday about finding the cameo. Another oddity in this strange old house.

The Bennett house had stood empty for five years before she and Arnold bought it. The last of the family, an old lady living in Massachusetts, had not visited for a decade before she passed on. A nephew put the house up for sale, contents included. The real estate agent was happy to pass their purchase offer to the nephew, who was quick to accept and hand over the keys.

Tucked into the Maple Grove Valley below a narrow ridge, the house faced a quiet road just inland from the Bay of Fundy. A few commuters passed early each morning, going to jobs in Parrsboro. Pickup trucks rumbled through on their way to pulp-cutting operations on the other side of Cape Chignecto.

Arnold worked at one of these operations, deep in the woods. It was too far to return home at the end of a shift.

"Are you sure you'll be all right, alone for five days at a time?" he'd asked, after he'd got the job with the Shulie pulp operation.

"I'll be fine. I'm used to being on my own. After all, think of the women whose husbands were away fighting in the Second World War. They were on their own for as much as six years. Nobody complained."

"Well, if you're sure...." He gave her a surreptitious glance. She was self-reliant, but with no family in the immediate area, she'd have to ask neighbours for any help she might need.

Now she saw him only between late Friday evening and Sunday evening. At the end of their brief visit, Arnold went to bed early, as he rose before dawn on Monday to drive the 40 miles to work.

In the morning, Vera looked at the cameo nestled in its box. She touched it. It was warm. The profile took on the delicate pink of living human flesh. Or could it be the sunlight reflecting off the rose quartz?

She phoned the museum.

"We do have pictures of the Bennett family," said the volunteer who answered the phone. "However, I'm not sure there will be enough detail for you to identify the cameo. I'm sorry to tell you we're closed until tomorrow. Mr. Collins, the curator, is at a conference."

Vera sighed and hung up the phone. Studying the pictures would have to wait. In the meantime, she decided to contact her old friend, Norbert Kelly, who lived 20 miles away in the village of Port Hebron. Norbert knew more than anyone about the people in this part of the county, their family connections, and their lives. His memory was incredible. He would certainly know the family, and maybe even have information about the woman who wore the cameo.

Norbert was delighted to hear from her.

"We'll have a good old chin-wag," he said. "I'll see you this afternoon, and I'll make a molasses cake to have with our tea. Bring that cameo, Vera. You've got me curious to see it now."

She put the cameo and a notebook in her backpack, hesitated a moment, and threw in a camera as well.

Vera drove slowly down the long, steep hill that ended at Port Hebron. There was plenty of time to get to Norbert's house, on the last street by the river. On an impulse, she suddenly decided to visit the United Church Cemetery, close to the junction with the main road to Port Hebron. She parked the Honda, and walked into the older section. Methodists and Presbyterians were laid to rest here, before most of those churches merged to form the United Church in 1925.

A wrought iron fence surrounded the graves which were laid out in neat rows and family plots under old maples and older willows. Trees whispered in a slight wind off the Bay. Stone angels marked the graves of children. The air felt chilly, even on this mid-

August day. Many tombstones bore the year 1918, the year of the Spanish Flu epidemic, including five Bennett graves.

Moss and a few faded plastic flowers covered some newer graves. Vera idly wondered how often relatives came to visit. She took a few pictures before getting back on the road.

Norbert was taking a warm molasses cake out of the oven when she came through the door. The tea steamed in a brown crockery pot on the woodstove. Vera greeted him with a hug, and sat at the kitchen table. She took out the small box, opened it, and held it out to her friend. She felt the heat of the cameo even through the box.

"Can you feel that?" she asked.

He looked bemused. "Feel what?"

"It's warm. At least it's warm when I pick it up."

Norbert had noticed nothing. He scrutinized the cameo, examining it from all angles. He gave her a long look, and handed it back to her.

"Where did you find this?" he asked.

"I found it at the back of a kitchen drawer. The pin caught in a rag." She stirred milk into her tea, and settled back with a slice of molasses cake. Norbert added sugar to his tea, and took a bite of cake.

"I don't suppose I told you about the first Bennetts to come around here," he said. "William Bennett came out from England with his parents as a child. Went to sea when he was a young man. In those days, all goods came across the ocean or along the coast. He travelled to England pretty often, the Mediterranean, China a time or two, South America—even went around the Horn. He'd come home every couple of years, always with trinkets for Gladys and the girls. Old William owned a schooner for a while. My father knew him well."

Norbert blew on his tea to cool it. William Bennett, he speculated, might have brought the cameo home, as a gift for Gladys or one of his daughters. He didn't recall seeing any of them wearing it, but fashion had changed by the time he was old enough to notice such things.

Norbert had been a boy of 15 at the time of the Spanish Flu so he remembered it, and its terrible toll on the village, vividly. Soldiers returning from the Great War had unknowingly brought home the infection. The flu spread like wildfire, striking down previously healthy people in only a day or two. They drowned in their own fluid-filled lungs, leaving stunned families to deal with their loss. Most were young men and women—not babies and old people epidemics usually took. Dozens of villages were abandoned, even their names now forgotten. Vera and Norbert had together visited several lost village sites. Nothing was left now but yellow daffodils around cellar holes, and country cemeteries with many crude wooden markers bearing the year 1918.

The Bennett family lost William first, then Gladys, then three daughters to the epidemic. Lucy, the youngest and only survivor, inherited the family home in which she and her husband Malcolm Wilbur lived with their two young children, before Malcolm was killed on a log drive. Two years after Malcolm's death, little James died of pneumonia. Lucy stayed on at the house with her daughter Evelyn. One year, she took her child to visit relatives in Boston, never to return. She wrote to a distant cousin, who agreed to act as caretaker of the Bennett house.

In the years afterwards, the cousin rented out the house to summer tenants. Evelyn came back occasionally for only a few weeks at a time, until she was too frail to travel.

Vera listened intently to Norbert's story. She imagined the widowed Lucy and her young daughter alone for days at a time, like herself, in the silent house.

She often felt the Bennetts had never left. The attic was chock-a-block with their things: trunks of clothing, boxes of postcards and books, a dressmaker's dummy, a spinning wheel, a tea-set from China, even a sewing machine with a heavy steel needle for sewing sails. Vera often spent rainy afternoons in the dusty space, reading postcards, trying on a dress from the Gay Nineties, and imagining community life in an earlier time.

In those days, the population was 10 times what it was now. Men fished, worked in the mills, cut timber in the woods like Arnold did now, but not near enough to come home often. Women raised large families and ran the farms in the men's absence. Gracious Victorian houses still dotted the countryside, the former homes of lumber barons, shipbuilders and prosperous farmers. The mansion of shipbuilder George Spicer, now an inn, even had a ballroom with polished hardwood floors. She'd applied for a waitress job there just a week ago.

Did Lucy Bennett wear the cameo to a dance at that home? Those were happy days, before the family was ravaged by the Spanish horror. Vera instinctively picked up the cameo from its little box.

Norbert noticed the gesture. "Something about that cameo speaks to you," he said.

She grinned sheepishly. "It does. Maybe because I'm surrounded by their stuff. I suppose we really should clean it out, especially the attic. It hasn't been touched in a good 50 years."

A burst of heat erupted from the cameo lying in her palm. It pulsed like a heartbeat. She dropped it, clattering, to the floor. Norbert's eyebrows lifted. Slowly, Vera picked up the cameo. Her jaw dropped. A spot of rosy colour highlighted the profile's cheek.

"Did you see that?" she asked. Norbert shook his head.

Without thinking, Vera hurriedly dropped the cameo in the box and clapped on the lid, covering the flushed cheek.

Norbert poured her another tea. "I think you might have stirred something up," he said carefully. "Or maybe something stirred you up."

Sensing her unease with the cameo, he suggested she leave it with him for a few days, at least until Arnold returned and the three of them could decide together what to do. Vera felt strangely reluctant to do so.

"I'll take it home," she said. "Whatever it is, it can't harm me. It's only a piece of jewellery."

Vera drove back with much on her mind. She made a simple dinner of fresh garden vegetables and cold ham, and listened to CBC Radio for an hour.

That night, she dreamed of a dance at the George Spicer house. Fireflies glimmered in the warm summer night. Young men and women waltzed to the strains of piano and violin. Guests spilled out of the brightly-lit room onto the lawn, laughing at a story. She heard a conversation, whispered urgently just under the sound of the music, but could not make out the words.

In the morning, Vera felt calmer. She glanced at the cameo. The profile shone white against the rose quartz. She touched the surface. It was cold—just inert stone.

She drove to the county museum, where the curator welcomed her to browse their photo collection. Within minutes, she found an album of the Bennett family, with captions in faded silver pencil. In one, William Bennett stood unsmiling with his hand on Gladys's shoulder. She held a baby on her knee, and a toddler clung to her hand. In another, little girls with giant hair ribbons posed demurely in front of a potted fern.

Vera turned the page, and swallowed. Here was the photo she remembered of the four Bennett daughters. The middle woman wore a high-necked shirtwaist blouse with a black ribbon around her neck, pinned with a cameo. Trembling, she rose from the table, and asked the volunteer to photocopy the picture for her. Vera drove home too fast, her mind full of questions.

Heavy rain the next morning meant no garden work, so she decided to spend a few hours poking around the attic. There might be clues in one of the trunks or wardrobes. She pulled the cord of a bare light bulb, creating a pool of light in the middle of the open room. Shadows danced on the walls. Outdoors, a sullen wind lashed rain on the old roof. The attic smelled of ancient mouse urine and a slight sour odour came from an old milk separator in a corner.

Vera pulled out a cotton high-necked shirtwaist with leg-of-mutton sleeves from a trunk. The fabric still smelled faintly of perspiration. An ankle-length skirt of fine wool lay folded beneath the shirtwaist. Both items appeared to be about her size. Faded velvet ribbons lay in a jumble on one of the trunk's papered shelves.

Suddenly inspired, she went downstairs and returned with the cameo in its box. She removed her tee-shirt and jeans, put on the shirtwaist and skirt, and tied a black ribbon around her neck. Vera twirled slowly, feeling the skirt brush the floor, imagining what it was like for whoever wore these clothes more than a century ago.

Nestled in its cotton wool bed, the cameo profile glowed rosy. It was warm. Vera picked it up, and tried to fasten it to the ribbon. She fumbled with the pin, missed the clasp, and poked the sharp tip under her fingernail. She cried out at the sudden pain, and the cameo tumbled onto the open trunk shelf. Blood welled up under her nail. A drop fell on the cameo's profile. She squeezed the finger in her other hand to stop the bleeding. Her heart pounded, and her face flushed.

A few minutes later, the blood stanched, Vera noticed a cheval mirror next to a jumble of bedroom furniture. It would be better to look in the mirror while she pinned on the cameo. She drew the mirror on its casters towards the light, and tipped it slightly to see herself full-length.

She tugged loose her ponytail, fastened the elastic just behind the top of her head and puffed her hair out around her face, mimicking the pompadour hairdos of the early 1900s. Her cheeks were still pink. Did they wear make-up in 1905? She smiled coquettishly at her reflection, imagining a young Lucy Bennett getting ready for a dance at the Spicer home, wondering if Malcolm Wilbur might be there.

Vera retrieved the cameo, and adjusted the mirror slightly so she could see to fasten the clasp. The light bulb swayed—probably a draft from a loose shingle. Something fuzzy obscured the image of the light bulb in the mirror. Puzzled, she looked more closely. In the mirror, she saw the hairdo, the black ribbon pinned with a cameo, but the face that looked back was not hers. It was a woman with fair hair and green eyes. She stared at Vera, her eyes wide. Vera stood frozen. The image slowly faded.

The light bulb swung from the rafter. It dimmed, and then flickered. The wind howled. She glanced through the window. Along the driveway, the old Lombardy poplars bent at a sharp angle in the driving rain. The barn door had lost one hinge and hung half-open. A sudden gust of wind banged it back against the barn wall. In the dim outline of the barn interior was a tall-wheeled shape. From here it looked like a buggy.

Vera pushed the mirror away from her, hurriedly pulled off the old clothing, and got dressed in her jeans and tee-shirt.

"I'm imagining things," she told herself. "Too much time on my hands. Wouldn't it be great to get that job at the Spicer Inn! I'd be busy and around lots of people. Maybe I could earn enough that Arnold wouldn't have to work so far away."

She slipped the cameo into her jeans pocket, and ran downstairs to find a kerosene lantern, candles and matches, in case the power went out.

In the evening, Arnold called to say he would not be coming home this weekend. Bad weather meant he had lost a day's pay, so he would work Saturday to make up the time. Vera sighed. Maybe she was alone too much. Arnold was a rock. He would reassure her that she wasn't going crazy. He had an analytical mind, and would surely come up with a reasonable explanation for the strange events that had gone on in the house.

She spent the rest of the day fiercely cleaning and making whole-wheat bread. House chores were a form of meditation, she thought. Nobody needs to think while vacuuming. By late afternoon, she was tired and ready for a break. Another solitary meal and a quick phone call to Norbert were the only markers in her day. Norbert had nothing new to offer about the cameo, but said he'd ask around the village about whatever happened to Lucy and Evelyn Wilbur.

The next morning brought some good news. Mary Reid, owner of the Spicer Inn, called to offer her a waitress job starting in a week.

"We've had a lot of reservations for the fall, and we need more staff," she said. "As usual, it's retired people who like to travel when it's not so busy on the highways and the weather's still nice. Even got bookings by some people in Germany. I was impressed that you'd taken German at university. They'll love having someone to serve them in their own language. The fall visitors tend to tip generously," she continued. "So even though we don't pay much, you'll still do well."

Vera accepted the job offer gladly. The extra money would help a lot. Maybe in a few years, she and Arnold could fix up the Bennett house and open a bed-and-breakfast. She hurried to call Norbert.

"Why, that's wonderful news, Vera. I've heard good things about Mary Reid. Runs a tight ship, but she's good to her staff. Most of them have been with her for years. Jobs are hard to find around here, especially ones that last long enough to get employment insurance in the winter."

Norbert had some news for her as well.

"I've asked around the village about Lucy and Evelyn Wilbur. Folks remember they had relatives in the Boston States, William's younger brother, Wesley, and his family. Wesley Bennett would be Lucy's uncle. His widow, Lily, and two of the boys spent a summer here back in the early '20s."

Norbert learned that the Boston Bennetts suffered the same devastation from the Spanish Flu as their cousins in Nova Scotia. As it had in Canada, the epidemic occurred in waves, racing through the population for several months, dying down, and then starting up again.

"The flu broke out just weeks after the boys came back from the Great War," he said. "Spread with the troop trains carrying all those discharged soldiers home. All the shipping traffic in and out of the Port of Boston—that carried the flu as well," Norbert said with a sigh. He paused a moment before continuing.

"I remember in the Halifax paper, they had stories about what happened in Boston. You know, there was a lot of back-and-forth traffic between Boston and Nova Scotia, going back to the early days."

Wesley Bennett was born in Canada, a few years after his parents and brother, William, emigrated from England. As an adult, Wesley moved to the outskirts of Boston, where he lived with his wife Lily and six children, two daughters and four sons. Only Lily and two boys were left after the flu hit. With the help of employees who survived the epidemic, they managed to carry on the family import-export business. Local people remembered Lily and her sons coming to Nova Scotia to spend a summer with Lucy and Evelyn, in the early 1920s.

"That's all I learned," Norbert finished. "The house was empty much of the time afterwards, though I do remember Evelyn spending a few summers here."

After making plans with Norbert for a visit the following week, Vera hung up the phone.

She suddenly had an idea. While going through a trunk in the attic, she had found a bundle of letters with Boston postmarks. Taking a small lamp, she climbed the worn attic stairs, and opened the trunk that held the letters. They bore cancellations dating from the early 1900s to 1923. She pulled out a letter from Mrs. Lily Bennett dated February 1919.

My dear Lucy,

We received your telegram with its terrible news. I am so sorry for your trouble. It is devastating to lose your dear sisters and both your parents so suddenly. We are still in shock after losing Wesley, my two precious girls and two of our dear boys, all just in a few months. It has shaken my trust in God. How could He want to take Papa and four innocent little children to Him? Everyone in Boston is asking these questions. So many are suffering.

In our city, we saw such sights as you could hardly imagine. The streets were silent. No one dared go out for fear of contamination. The telephone exchanges are closed, since so many operators are sick or have died. Theatres, workplaces, restaurants—

all closed. The churches have even limited funerals to 15 minutes, since there are so many every day, and also out of fear of contagion.

Dear Lucy, try to have faith that we will get through this awful epidemic. We can only hope to see our loved ones again in a better place.

Our house feels lonely now, without the children's laughter and Wesley's cheerful, "Hello!" when he arrives home from work. Do give a thought to come to us for a long visit, perhaps even to stay permanently. It would do my heart good.

Wishing you comfort in your sorrow,
Your loving aunt, Lily Bennett.

The last letter was dated 1923 and postmarked Boston. In it, Lucy Wilbur wrote to her cousin in Parrsboro, with directions to advertise the house for rent to long-term tenants.

Vera slowly put the letter down, and re-tied the ribbon around the bundle. She hoped the two widows had been able to comfort each other.

Later, she carried out her usual evening ritual. She wiped down the table, the counter tops and stove, rinsed and wrung out the cloth, and left it to hang on the stove door handle. Vera wondered how many women before her had repeated the same familiar chores. The house dated to the mid-nineteenth century, so it could be six or seven generations. In her mind's eye, she saw a parade of women who had lived in this house, birthed their children, laughed and loved much, cared for the ill and dying, mourned their dead, and grew old themselves.

She glanced at the window above the sink, and noticed a full moon shining through broken clouds. Maybe Lucy Wilbur had stood at this counter-top, perhaps in the same clothing she herself had tried on. Dreamily, she pulled the cameo from her pocket, and held it up to her throat. In the window, an image formed. Someone was standing behind her. She whirled around.

Between her and the stairs stood a woman, her eyes wide in horror. The woman raised a hand across her mouth. Her breath came in shallow gasps. She stared uncomprehendingly at Vera. She looked as if…she'd seen a ghost.

Vera stared back. The woman wore a high-necked shirtwaist and a long wool skirt. Her fair hair was pulled back from her face with little tendrils escaping around her ears. A black velvet band circled her neck. Pinned to it was a rose cameo. Its twin pulsed in Vera's grasp, scorching her fingers. It slipped from her hand, clattered across the floor, and tumbled into a gap by the wall.

Instinctively, Vera flung her apron over her face to shield her eyes from the apparition. She stood rigidly for several minutes. Slowly, she dropped her apron. The woman was gone. The clock struck 11 p.m. The house was quiet. There was no sign of the cameo.

~~~***~~~

The House on the Hill
Janet Doleman

On a cool, late April night, while the moon shone weakly through a veil of clouds, seven of us crowded into the confines of a '67 Ford station wagon with worn upholstery, an intermittent heater and a stubborn clutch. Phil, the sole holder of a driver's license in the group, managed to get his father's car on Friday nights. Along with one other boy, Eddie, were five girls: me (Janey), Rosemary, Maria, Eliza, and Patty, Phil's younger sister. All of us were forbidden to date solo, or to drive in cars with boys, or attend unsupervised parties. The exceptions to the "boys" rule were Phil, who was the Baptist minister's son, and Eddie, whose dad was the new CO of the nearby Air Force base, and thereby approved as suitable company. Our parents believed that both boys' every action was safely approved and monitored by the respective fathers, and any untoward behaviour was sniffed out and duly dealt with. Our collective parents appeared to have agreed upon an acceptable code of conduct for their assorted offspring, and seemed to possess a telepathic knowledge of our actions and whereabouts. We called it telepathic but we knew that the old busybodies of the village, like Mrs. Dawse, made it their life's goal to know everyone else's business. There was no escaping.

Except for us. We deemed ourselves under the radar as long as we didn't blab to our parents or, heaven forbid, to our younger siblings. They took it as their family duty to report every action to our parents, unless, of course, they held back juicy tidbits to use as blackmail for their own advantage.

On this chilly April night, safe, stalwart Phil, eager as the rest of us for an adventure at the end of a dull week of school and homework, parked the car at the head of the beach road on the landward side of the island, doused the headlights, and left us in near darkness, illuminated slightly by the moon's glow.

The beach curved in an outward arc towards the mainland, its tip pointing at the rocky causeway connecting the island to the mainland. That was where our village strung out along both sides of a two-lane road, bordered by the railway tracks along the shoreline on one side and woods on the other.

"Are we going to check out the parking lot?" piped up Eddie. "Or maybe we can jump the dunes?"

The dunes were our version of a playground, especially on nights like this, with each of us feeling the need for freedom from restrictions, when we could act childishly without being criticized by anyone outside our circle.

"I don't know," said Maria. "It's too dark to see the path." Maria often dampened our enthusiasm with expressions of caution and restraint.

Adventure in our world was tempered by the fear of getting caught if we dared to commit a rash act. Stealing property, breaking windows, or inadvertently hurting someone was declared off-limits. Borrowing property, on the other hand, was acceptable, as long as the said item was restored to its former owner and location at the end of the night.

Rosemary spoke up. "We could sneak up on Bud Smith and Marilyn and give them a good scare. I think they've gone parking down by the dunes tonight."

Tucked behind the sand dunes at the end of the gravelled road, lay a sandy clearing big enough to hold half a dozen cars. On a sunny day, it would be filled with mothers unloading their assorted children, folding chairs, picnic baskets and beach toys for an afternoon on the beach. It was nearly empty after five o'clock, except after dark on weekends, which was a popular time for couples to park at the end farthest from the lone street lamp, the feeble glow unable to reach into a car's interior.

That end of the lot could be treacherous for cars whose tires would spin helplessly, digging deeper into the sand. This was common knowledge in the area. Even so, the risk of becoming marooned with no one to help push the car out if it got stuck was tempered by the promise of privacy for parking couples.

"How do we scare them? And what with?" asked Eliza who could be counted on to equip our "team". We had forgotten to establish a plan that night, much to Eliza's disappointment.

"Why don't we get a barrel of fish bait over at Long Wharf, creep up to the car, and dump it over the windshield?" offered Eddie.

Our little community gained its livelihood from the fishing industry of Cape Sable Island and surrounding villages, hence the prolific presence of boats, fishing gear, and barrel upon barrel of smelly, disgusting fish bait. Usually, we did not dare go near wharves or wharf buildings, under threat of grounding from our parents, who warned us repeatedly with stories of young children drowning off the end of wharves. We respected their experience and directives after hearing those tragic tales.

Rosemary, ever practical, dismissed this idea. "Those barrels are too heavy, and smelly. Besides, we'd have to heave one in the back of the car to get it here, and the stink would be inside for weeks and maybe months. Can you imagine Rev. Bob coming to church smelling like fish?"

Living where we did, especially when the wind changed before a nor'easter, meant we were familiar with the horrible smell associated with rotting fish entrails.

"We don't even know if their car is parked there," added Patty. "One of us should sneak down to check the parking lot."

"Eddie?" we all said together.

"I know, okay, okay, I'll do it. It's always me who gets the go-fer jobs," grumbled Eddie good-naturedly. Eddie, slight for his age but extremely agile, was routinely expected to scale fences and sneak into backyards on behalf of the group.

On a knoll high above the beach stood the old Robertson house. Cradled by overgrown spruce and wildly unkempt alder bushes, its peaked roof was split by the sharp point of a dormer, and un-curtained windows stared blankly over the bay and sandy shoreline. In the daylight, the paint-peeling storm door with its single eye of a diamond-shaped pane was barred against intruders either human or weather-related. The house stood benignly amongst the grasses and overgrown bushes. Tonight, its presence was obscured by darkness. We were aware of the house but were not thinking about it particularly.

Stories of ghostly sightings at the old Robertson house had been absorbed into local lore. Some said it once belonged to a sea captain engaged in trading between the Boston states, the West Indies and the colony of Newfoundland. He sailed away for four or five years at a time leaving his wife to fend for herself and her children. When news arrived that his ship was lost at sea, the widow packed up her family and fled the island for her relatives on the mainland. Locals said they used to see a light from the upstairs window long after the family left. It was speculated that the sea captain had returned, not dead after all, but back to claim his wife and family. Grieved that he could not find them, it was rumoured that he took up residence on the top floor, although no one ever saw him during the day.

Yet another story circulated that the house had once been inhabited by a young boy who lived there with his grandfather, a tyrant who used to beat his grandson for little or no reason. When the grandfather died suddenly, whispers drifted around the community about the young boy who, terrorized beyond reason, was driven to commit murder. The boy was sent away in the care of a distant aunt and uncle, the house boarded up and left empty. No evidence of foul play was ever discovered or reported, despite abundant rumours. Long years later he returned, not to the house, but to a little shack behind the railway station. He was referred to locally as Ol' Man Thorburn. He was seen every week buying his bread, milk, and tins of cat food for the numerous cats living at his shack, barely mumbling five words before shuffling back down Station Road, clutching his paper grocery bag.

Rosemary told us a third version, learned from her 98-year-old grandmother. The Acadian fishermen, who for years sailed into the bay in the spring to fish, erected simple houses to live in during the summer months. Eventually, they formed a settlement. The men dried their catch on raised pole platforms along the shore while their wives dug small garden plots for growing vegetables and hung their wet laundry on the bushes to dry. This version, and the two previous, were likely all true, given the historic timeline.

The British drove out the Acadian families in the mid-1700s, scattering them as far as Louisiana territory. Some of them escaped beforehand in small boats, hiding in the woods farther up along the shore to the west, while others were rounded up and put on ships bound for Boston. Their former lands were bestowed on hardy souls out of Nantucket, who arrived on this rocky coast somewhat dismayed at the lack of rich soil for establishing farms. Instead, they learned to rely on the sea: fishing, boatbuilding, and trading by ship. Hence the sea captain story, which could have taken place at any point between 1767 and 1900. Ol' Man Thorburn, of an indeterminate age given his severely wrinkled face and stooped posture, could easily have grown up in the early twentieth century, giving credence to the abusive grandfather story.

The old Robertson house was probably around 200 years old, being of frame construction and similar to a Cape Cod style. Symmetrically placed windows flanked the extended covered entrance at the front, where the battened storm door stood firm. None of us remembered ever seeing signs of anyone living in the house. There were no curtains at the windows, no lights at night, only a path beaten down in the grass by Alfred Nolan, the elderly caretaker.

We had long since lost interest in the house. Our list of forbidden places included the old Robertson place, which, we were warned, had an unmarked well somewhere on the grounds. I was not anxious to fall down an abandoned well; in fact, it gave me nightmares if I allowed myself to think about it. The well had been filled with rocks and other debris, we were told.

Time passed. We were beginning to feel the cold after sitting in the car with the engine off, no matter how crowded together we were. No one had thought to bring a thermos of hot chocolate or a candy bar. It would soon be time to head for home, and we hadn't even decided on what to do. Eddie had not returned from his spy mission.

"We're going to have to—" Eliza started to speak, but was interrupted by a distinct *CRASH!*

We all jumped as one body.

"What was that?" ventured Patty in a tiny voice.

No one answered her until Rosemary said, very quietly, "It sounded like—"

CRASH! We heard it again. Maria let out a whimper, like a small puppy.

"That sounded like something heavy," said Phil, "like a club or a mallet or—"

"Or a what?" whispered Eliza.

Another crash sounded, louder than the last.

"Maybe it's Eddie, playing tricks on us," said Rosemary firmly, although we detected a faint tremor in her voice. "He's the only one around, unless there's someone down in the parking lot, and they'll be too busy to make those noises."

At that moment, we heard running footsteps and Eddie's face appeared in the side window.

"Open the door! Open the door!" His tone was frantic. Maria opened the door and Eddie dived in, heedless of where he landed on us. Maria quickly pushed the lock down on the door. Eddie scrambled to sit up and catch his breath.

"Did you hear that?" he asked, gulping and panting. "Did you hear that noise?"

"Yup, we heard it all right," declared Phil. "We thought it might be you doing it."

"No way! Are you kidding?" asked Eddie. "I was down by the parking lot, crawling up the first dune to scope it out, and this huge crashing sound came from behind me. I nearly jumped outta my skin!"

"Behind you?" asked Rosemary, who liked to clarify things to their very marrow. "That means it came from up by the old Robertson house."

"But nobody's been up there for years!" said Eddie. He paused. "Or at least, that's what everyone says."

"Who is 'everyone'?" asked Maria. "Maybe someone lives there secretly, like the old sea captain...."

"He'd be about 150 years old," scoffed Eliza. "I don't think so!"

"What about his ghost though, the one who lives in the attic," suggested Maria. "Ghosts don't age like humans, they live on and on."

"Yeah," said Eddie, recovering from his shakiness. "They just keep wandering around forever, until someone kills them again. Maybe the noise is from the ghost houses the French people lived in. When they were burned, the roofs would've collapsed and crashed in."

"Well," said Rosemary, "I'm not so sure I believe in ghosts, whoever they are, or were... but that noise was very real, and I think we should find out what caused it."

"You're joking, right?" asked Maria and Patty together. "Why doesn't Phil start up the car and we all get out of here, right now!"

"Well, we came for an adventure, so why not check it out? There are seven of us. If we all go together, and take whatever we can find as weapons, we'll be able to protect ourselves," insisted Rosemary.

"I don't know," began Maria. "What if...we run into...." Her voice faltered, unable to put her fears into words.

"Phil, what's in the trunk?" asked Eliza, ready to take on the challenge of equipping warriors for battle. "A jack? Tools? Maybe a flashlight?"

"Uh, I'll go check." He hesitated before opening his door, and quickly moved around to open the tailgate. The rest of us kept a vigilant watch, straining our eyes into the darkness around the car. The moon remained stuck behind clouds, ineffectual. Phil struggled with the catch on the wheel well, and finally wrenched it open.

"A spare tire, tire iron, jack, and a small screwdriver," said Phil, handing forward items that might be useful as weapons. He closed the hatch and the tailgate, and scurried back to the driver's seat, locking the door as he slid behind the wheel.

"There's nothing else?" asked Eliza. "No boards or shovel or anything?"

"Nope," said Phil, "My dad cleared it all out last weekend."

We divided up the tools. They didn't amount to much if effective weaponry might be required.

"I guess I could poke out its eye with this screwdriver," Eliza held up her weapon, eyeing it doubtfully. "That is, if ghosts have eyes."

"We don't know that was a ghost," Rosemary said, keeping her voice even. "What we are going to do is leave the car at the same time, and walk slowly up the lane towards the house. If we stick together, it will look like we're really big, instead of one puny person who's easy to take down."

I found my voice at last. "What about the well?" I asked. "How are we going to see the well in the dark? One false step and one of us could just slip in."

"That well was filled in years ago, and if we stick to the lane, there's no chance we'll even go near it." Phil's words were only mildly reassuring.

"So, are we ready?" asked Rosemary, wielding the tire iron with both hands. "I'll lead and Phil will bring up the rear. If anyone sees or hears anything, grab the arm of the person nearest you and stop in your tracks. Don't run, whatever you do."

"That's for bears, not ghosts," said Patty. "Even *I* know that."

"Oh, great," I said. "Now we have to worry about bears, wells, *and* ghosts."

"C'mon, all of you, let's go now!" urged Rosemary. She set off, trailed by Eliza, Maria, Patty, Eddie, and me, then Phil, so close he was stepping on my heels.

We tried to walk quietly along the road, gravel crunching under our feet, until we reached the entrance to the lane leading up the hill. Suddenly, there was a whirring sound, which escalated to a high pitched whine.

"What is that?" shrieked Maria, clutching the girls next to her so hard they flinched.

"I think it's a car spinning its tires in the sand," answered Eddie. "Someone went parking tonight after all!"

"Shouldn't we go help them? Maybe we can push them out?" suggested Maria, who was ready for any diversion away from the house on the hill.

The sound of a car engine grew louder and closer. Our eyes were blinded by headlights.

"Watch out!" yelled Eddie, as he tried to drag us out of the way. We scrambled off the gravel in time to avoid being grazed by the careering car, clearly identified as Bud Smith's Chev by the amount of chrome on its sides as it streaked past us. We could just glimpse the top of Marilyn's blonde bouffant hair before the red taillights disappeared around a bend.

"He didn't even see us!" exclaimed Eddie. "Wonder why he was going so fast?"

The words were no sooner out of his mouth when a prolonged dragging noise reached our ears. We slowly turned around, just as the stubborn clouds broke open and moonlight lit up the front of the house on the hill. We gasped aloud. The bar on the storm door was ripped off, the door swinging back erratically. That explained the banging noises. A tall figure appeared to be dragging a big box or trunk, bent over and lurching as if it was very heavy. He was dragging it in the direction of the beach.

Without looking at each other, we turned and ran as one, reached the car, and grabbed wildly at the door handles before throwing ourselves inside. Phil fumbled with the keys, started the engine, and turned the car towards the village, not even looking around to see if we were all there.

After several minutes, Rosemary spoke. "Okay, that was scary. Even I have to admit it."

"Who do you think that was?" asked Eddie. "The sea captain? Mr. Nolan?"

"Not Mr. Nolan. He's too old, too short, and no way could he pull that much weight." Phil snorted. "And it wasn't the sea captain. At least not the one you're thinking about."

"Shouldn't we tell someone?" Maria's mild voice was barely audible.

"We can't tell anyone, because then we'll be in real trouble. You know that we're not supposed to go near that place. If our folks find out, we're all done for."

"Let's just go home," said Eliza. "I've had enough adventure for one night."

***

Across the bay from the beach, Mrs. Dawse was adjusting her curtains at the front window before retiring for the night, when she noticed a glint of light in the distance.

"There's a light on in the old Robertson house," she mused. "That's odd."

***

The next morning, Mrs. Dawse telephoned to make sure my mother knew about Bud Smith's abrupt departure for Ontario to work at an automobile plant with his uncle, and about the light coming from the old Robertson house the night before. My mother repeated the whole conversation to me as she resumed her weekly Saturday baking ritual.

Preoccupied as she was with her task, she wasn't aware of my rapt attention to each detail. There was no mention of Bud's girlfriend Marilyn.

***

Later that same morning, Phil called. He and Patty arrived home the night before to see their father, Rev. Bob, standing on the doorstep. He was dressed in his weekday sports jacket, shirt and tie, looking at his watch under the porch light. Phil handed him the car keys.

"Tell your mother that I have to go to the hospital, and I'm not sure how late I'll be," said Rev. Bob. "I just got a call from Martha Nolan; Alfred Nolan's had a stroke."

Phil and Patty looked at each other wordlessly as their dad drove away.

***

That Sunday afternoon, when Mrs. Crosby from the United Church took a tinfoil-covered plate of dinner to Ol' Man Thorburn's little house, as was her habit, she noticed that the cats were all outside the door, mewling and looking hungrily at the plate she carried. When her repeated knocking got no response, she hurried off to fetch Mr. Crosby. He quickly returned with Rev. Bob, and they forced the lock to find Ol' Man Thorburn unconscious on his cot, an uneaten meal from the day before still laid out on the table. He was taken to the hospital but never regained consciousness, and died before the week was out. Only the minister and a handful of mourners attended the funeral. No one could remember any family ever visiting Ol' Man Thorburn.

The shack stood empty for a while and the cats took up residence under the station platform. Maria's father, who was the station agent, put out food scraps and saucers of milk for them. Eventually, the town council declared the shack an eyesore, and decided to raze it. The few belongings worth saving were stacked in an unused storeroom at the railway station in case relatives of Ol' Man Thorburn showed up to claim them. Pushed into the far corner of the storeroom was a big metal trunk with a curved top and rusting hinges. A big padlock hung off the front, and affixed to the outside were faded, barely legible labels, reading "Boston", and "...ntego Bay". Piled on top of the trunk were an iron bed frame, old chairs, and cardboard boxes.

***

As time went on, the events of that night became less important, and our attention was focused in other directions. Our little group dispersed. Maria and Phil started dating. The rest of us, even Patty, were not welcome on their jaunts in Phil's father's car. Eddie's dad was posted to another base in Quebec. Eliza and Rosemary decided they wanted to pursue nursing careers, and volunteered for the Candy Striper's program at the regional hospital.

In my free time, I escaped the house to take our family dog on long walks to the shore. While Trixie explored the rock pools and stalked hermit crabs, I perched on a boulder where I could gaze across the bay at the old Robertson house. My imagination invented scenarios of what might have taken place within those walls over the many years it stood empty.

The scouring salty winds continued to batter the old house, until little of its green paint remained. Eventually, new caretakers took over, cutting down the scraggly trees and bushes, mowing the grass, and drilling a brand-new well so the house could be rented. However, potential renters didn't stay longer than a couple of weeks, complaining that the house was perpetually cold. There were renewed rumours of odd noises from the closed-off attic.

As was the custom, rumours and stories faded into the local lore, and many forgot the events of that early spring. Trains ran less frequently along the shore, eventually stopping altogether, and the railway station was boarded up. Ol' Man Thorburn was remembered as a reclusive, quirky old man, but few people could say they actually knew him. His belongings gathered dust in the station storeroom, where they were forgotten until, one night, someone noticed flames leaping from the station roof. By the time the volunteer fire department arrived to hose down what remained, the roof had caved in, and little of the structure remained. Maria's father, now retired, volunteered to help clear away the debris once the fire investigation was complete. When questioned, he didn't remember seeing a trunk in the ruins. He told Maria a metal trunk like that wouldn't burn up. The raised train platform looked incongruous without the building behind it, like the ghost of an era when trains thundered daily into the station, screeching to a stop to disgorge passengers and freight.

***

A few short years later, I returned home to visit my mother. One day, I walked along the old railway line, now bereft of iron rails and tar-blackened ties, in the direction of the causeway. At a place where there was a wide view of the bay between clumps of trees, I paused to look across at the beach. Perched atop the bluff where the old Robertson house had been stood a huge, multi-storied house, like a modern-day castle, multiple roof lines and dormers placed to catch every angle of the sun and sea breezes, no doubt with a sophisticated air-conditioning system for back-up. With landscaped grounds, neatly trimmed grass and ornamental trees placed precisely around the perimeter, it was state-of-the-art, as if whisked from the pages of a home design magazine and plopped onto the pristine lot. No signs of the old house remained. I felt a pang of nostalgia for the old house of my younger days, which breathed history as well as mystery from its every corner and cranny.

When I returned to my mother's place, I paused in the doorway to marvel at her fortitude; she still prided herself on remembering dates and names of people she knew from childhood.

"I noticed a new house over by the beach," I said, "on the spot where the old Robertson house used to be. Do you know who lives there?"

"Let me see." She tilted her head to one side, as if searching her memory. "I recall Melanie telling me—you remember Melanie, don't you? Mrs. Dawse's daughter?—about a man and his wife showing up out of the blue, going straight to that spot on the hill, bound and determined they were going to build a house overlooking the beach, and not even bothering to look at other properties. Before anyone knew it, the old house was gone, and that monstrosity sprang up almost overnight. Five bathrooms! Imagine!"

I waited.

"Their name is... it's something like Thornton or Thornbloom or... hmm...." She looked up and tapped her chin as if that would help her remember the name.

"Thorburne!" she said suddenly. "That's it. Thorburne, with an 'e' on the end. They were adamant about the spelling. Definitely not from around here, perhaps down around Boston way? Or New York? They must be, to have that much money!" She raised her eyebrows and inclined her head towards me, as if suggesting the solution to a puzzle.

"Oh," she added, "they also have a fancy sailboat, but bigger, more like a yacht. It's usually anchored in the cove next to the beach, but they just left on a trip around the world. Melanie called this morning to catch me up on the news."

I thought of the mysterious disappearance of the old trunk before the station fire. What if... my mind raced with scenarios. Could Bud Smith have been the tall figure we saw that night, dragging the trunk to the beach and loading it in a boat? He'd disappeared the next day, presumably to Ontario to work. Was it really Marilyn we saw driving recklessly past us on the beach road? Had Bud been in a conspiracy with Alfred Nolan, the caretaker? Or with Ol' Man Thorburn? Did Ol' Man Thorburn have family connections after all, and had their descendants now taken up residence in the brand-new house? The possibilities surged and clamoured to the surface of my mind for attention.

What if the trunk had been hidden away in the attic of the house on the hill for years and years, until that fateful, chilly April night? Was it a treasure chest left behind by the sea captain? I thought of how afraid we'd been of seeing ghosts in the old Robertson house.

This was so much more interesting than mere ghosts.

~~~***~~~

The Dancing Tulip
Wilma Stewart-White

She drove deeper and deeper into the forest. The trees arched over her closer and closer. Perhaps this was a wild goose chase. She was collecting information for her research on old houses of Lunenburg County and her friend, Martha, had enthused about an early house she said she had lived in as a child. She was following Martha's instructions and had turned at the old Baptist church on the corner. The road had quickly branched and narrowed.

What had been a pretty little country road with a cosy tunnel of green was turning into a very narrow lane that now squeezed the car tighter and tighter. Branches reached out, leaving fingernail scratches on the roof.

Why am I doing this? she wondered. *I can blame Martha.*

"Hmmm," she finally said in frustration, thinking about how she would talk to Martha. "If this road peters out and I'm stuck with nowhere to turn, I'll scream. I've started too late in the day. This path is dark and gloomy and the day is wearing on."

Suddenly, the tunnel ceased and the car shot out, released from the thicket of branches. The sun, close to setting, glared right in her face, momentarily blinding her. She jammed on the brake and took stock of her surroundings. She got a quick glance of a barred gate in front of her and a huge red barn on a hill. Two black and white sheepdogs raced to the gate, barking, daring her to come closer.

"You! Vat you vant?"

She jumped half out of her skin.

A gnarled old man peered in her window. Where had he come from?

She tried to quickly gather her wits about her. She looked at the caricature of a face. Two small, evil, glowing eyes glared at her.

Skinny hands with long curving fingernails left a trace of slime on her window. She inched her window down hesitantly.

"I am doing research on old buildings around here and I was told there was such a house here. I am interested in seeing it."

"Of course, is old but is private house—no visitors."

"Oh, well—you see, I am also looking for traces of early Lunenburg County symbols. I hear you have a rare carving. I only wanted a quick look and maybe a photo…?"

Inwardly, she quailed at the thought of actually getting out of the safety of her car and coming face to face with this creature and his two snarling dogs. Was she mad?

"Komm then."

He wrenched open the gate and whistled to the dogs.

Slowly, she edged her way up the deeply rutted track to a house so old it seemed rooted in the hillside. Up close, the barn seemed even more enormous. A flock of dirty, unshorn sheep moved steadily closer, watching her out of small, dark eyes.

She slowly opened the car door. The flock parted unwillingly, providing a walkway to the house. The house was indeed old with a low roof and tiny windows. The door was almost sunk into the earth. The gnome appeared and ushered her in, swiftly closing the door behind her

The room was almost pitch dark. She blinked and tried to focus. A fetid earthy and mouldy smell filled her nostrils. A massive hearth faced the door and a miserable fire glowered in the grate. A huge wooden table took pride of place heaped with onions and cabbage and potatoes. Carrots lay in a separate pile. They seemed to be in curious shapes, almost as if they had legs. A pile of old pewter plates sat at the other end of the table beside a large black pot and a wicked looking knife.

"Here!" he shouted. "Iss this vat you vanted to see?" He pointed to a carving on the mantle.

The date, 1762, and the name, Johan Schlangenveit, was engraved and beside it a beautifully carved tulip. The tulip, though frozen in time, was bent ever so slightly, petals fanned, as if it had been blown by a gentle breeze.

The "dancing tulip" was a well-loved symbol of the early settlers from Germany. They were also occasionally seen on some of the earliest slate gravestones. They were rare and were similar to ones found in Lancaster County, Pennsylvania, whose settlers were also from small villages along the Rhine. Links between Lunenburg and Pennsylvania were rare. This carving was well executed and very delicately done.

"Oh," she gasped. "How lovely."

The gnome smiled, showing his very unlovely teeth. He seemed pleased with her response. "Yah. His land, his house he built and his farm from the beginning ven ve all came from the old country. Even though ze tried to push him out. Tried to scare him avay. Vild horses at full of moon."

What on earth was he talking about, she wondered. *Wild horses?* Then she remembered the rest of Martha's spooky tale. The settler family who had lived there told stories of the house being haunted by a troop of marauding Indians. Many people, though, thought the ghosts were settlers in disguise trying to scare the inhabitants away.

"Alvays a full moon zey ride, zey whoop—but I not afraid—iss my home alvays."

His eyes strayed to a small door beside the hearth. The door was very narrow and low, almost too small for anyone today. In fact, it looked perfect for the gnome. She looked at it more closely. An ancient, hand-forged latch was well worn. His eyes followed.

"Does this door open?" she asked

"*Nein*, always locked. Zere iss no key. Opens by itself ven moon is full and horses come. Staircase goes down to old cellar below the earth. No one ever goes zere."

"So the door goes to the cellar?"

"*Nein*, much deeper"

His eyes slid away from hers—evasive and secretive.

This sounded highly implausible. She began to wonder what was actually going on here. She knew it would be wise to leave this curious place. "I think I should go. Could I take a picture of your lovely tulip carving?"

He screwed up his eyes, then reluctantly said, "Yah, ok but yust tulip."

"Thank you." She smiled and snapped a few shots, wishing she could also capture him and his funny door.

"How long have you lived here?"

"Many, many years. Not many people come. Iss sad house with many bad things zat happen here. No one else vants to be here."

"It is a lovely property with such a big barn that sits so high on the hill. You could see for miles," she said

"Alvays dying in ze barn—sheep vont go in."

This was getting too creepy. She edged to the door. He slipped past her and opened the outside door a tiny bit. She had to edge past him to get out.

She looked back at the ancient door and saw above it another carving. It was round and had strange markings on it. Suddenly, she realized it was a rare, old country hex symbol. They were put above doorways to protect against witches and evils unknown, even in the new world.

She stood under the symbol for a moment feeling a sense of its power and hesitated for a moment, but the urge to move propelled her on. The strong odour of earth and mustiness wreathed around him. He leaned back against the door and peered at her with curious eyes.

She could feel him looking deep inside her and she shivered. All around the old door latch were deep scratches. She looked again at his curled hands with the long nails.

Tiny bottle-glass panes of the windows, aglow with stray rays from the setting sun, gave the house a sly look. The landscape around was darkening, shadows were lengthening. The barn seemed afloat as a slight mist rose from behind it.

There was no sign of any other person.

"Do you live here alone? You are a long way from the main road."

"Zere iss only me. I live here always and alone. But tonight I vill haff many visitors. It iss the full of the moon. Zey will be here soon. Do you vish to see? You could some back and see?"

His fingers curled and his eyes gleamed.

"No. No thank you. You have been very kind."

She hurried back to the car and, with difficulty, turned in the yard. The barn loomed behind her. The evening mists were rising still higher. Through her rear window, she could look right through the open barn doors at the moon just beginning to rise. Were her eyes playing tricks? She could see figures in the higher levels of the barn.

"Oh, God," she whimpered.

The figures were hanging from the beams, slowly twisting. The gnome moved slowly towards the car. She locked the doors and quickly shot down the yard.

Suddenly, he appeared and swung the gate open with a horrible screech.

How did he get here so fast? she wondered.

She had almost reached the lane of trees. Just before she entered, she looked back over her shoulder. The full moon hung higher in the sky, but the house and barn had disappeared. She heard and faint pattering of horses' hooves and weird whooping calls. She shot down the lane as fast as she could, disregarding the tree roots and grabbing branches. Behind her, the trees swallowed up the dirt road. You couldn't even tell it was there.

Her digital camera glowed and flashed a tantalizing rectangle of light from the passenger seat.

Did it hold the secret tulip within?

~~~***~~~

Graveyard Study

Tom Robson

Before leaving school one October afternoon, Ms. Williams, the Grade Four teacher at my school, sought my approval for yet another of her excellent teaching ideas. "Mr. Robson, I'm thinking of taking my class to do a graveyard study."

She hesitated, perhaps looking for signs of disapproval or trying to anticipate my reaction.

She went on to explain how it fitted with the study of pioneers and settlers, and how the graveyard she had in mind had some interesting turn of the twentieth century markers.

She did not know that I enjoyed graveyards, especially those which served small, rural communities such as the one she was describing. I knew they could reveal a wealth of information and pose questions which students of all ages could research.

If she'd known of my interest, she would not have been concerned. I approved her trip instantly and asked if I could accompany her and the class there. A date was set and the plan was put in motion.

It was surprising that I had never stopped to investigate the particular cemetery she wanted to visit, even though I drove past it twice every working day going to and from school. It looked too small and insignificant to be interesting. The white and black trimmed, wooden church it surrounded was no longer in regular use. Ms. Williams had told me about the graves of the local, landowning family who had built the church, and of the large number of memorials to children. She had pricked my interest.

Later that same afternoon, I pulled into the small driveway at the church to wander among the gravestones. There was much that children could learn from these markers and I decided to make some notes of things they could focus on.

It was October and there was a fall chill in the air. I spent longer there than I intended, deciphering fading inscriptions and reading about the landowning family, whose exploits were written on their memorial stones. Not only had the family built the church and given the land for the graveyard more than 100 years before, they had also employed many of those buried there. Though I knew that children's graves were a sad feature of many cemeteries of this era, this one seemed to have far more than its share: too many dating from the 1918 flu epidemic.

Dark clouds, a strengthening breeze, and an awareness that I was late heading home, sent me back to the car. As I passed the church, set on the edge among some trees, I tried to identify an indistinct noise I could hear in the wind. It seemed to be coming from inside the church, though I knew it was locked and seldom used since the consecration of the new one, a few miles down the road. I stood and listened, but could separate nothing from the sound of wind in the trees.

Over the next few days, I did some research on the church. I discovered that the landowner had been involved in immigration in the 1870s.

Records showed that General Laurie, who had his town house on Morris Street as well as his estate at Oakfield, had brought out three families of "agricultural labourers with their 17 children" on the SS *Hibernian* in August of 1873.

He was also responsible for the placement of 76 "destitute children" arriving on the same ship, brought from Mrs. Rye's emigration home in England by a Mrs. Birt. In April of the next year, the same lady arrived, again on the *Hibernian*, with close to 80 children, ages four to 16. General Laurie had the responsibility of "distributing" these "Home Children" to families throughout Nova Scotia.

He discontinued this work soon after, possibly because of the criticism that annually, in Halifax, there were "at least 50 little ones dying from starvation in the hands of 'nurses'." A writer in the Halifax Evening Reporter urged that this problem be addressed rather than using our resources on imported waifs and strays.

Intrigued by this additional knowledge, I wanted to revisit the graveyard to verify some inscriptions. I also wanted to look inside the small church where, I was told, hung some plaques commemorating the general and his sons. I arranged to borrow the key from the caretaker and stopped by on my way home from school.

Again it was a late afternoon, darkened by overhanging, threatening clouds sent scurrying across the sky by chilly winds. I sought the information I needed from grave markers, hurrying to beat the threatening rain.

I closely checked two family markers. On each were recorded the births and early deaths of four children. I confirmed that these eight children were likely those of estate workers brought to Canada by the general.

When the storm began and the rain came, I sought shelter, and further information, inside the church. I unlocked the door and, as I stepped into the entrance way, I heard the same noise that I thought I'd imagined on my previous visit.

Someone was definitely crying, and it was coming from inside the church.

Nervously, I peeked into the chancel. There were about 12 rows of carved, wooden pews. Towards the front sat a woman, head bowed and body racked with sobs. Between the sobs I could hear her anguished words, "Why? Why? Why?"

I knew there had been a burial in the churchyard the previous week. I thought I must be intruding on someone's private grief at that loss. Without making my presence known, I retreated. I felt so sorry for the woman and would have liked to help, but couldn't. It didn't seem right.

As I discreetly closed the church door behind me, I heard more words punctuating the cries. I could only distinguish, "my babies, my babies...." as the wind and the rain muffled the voice.

I got into my car and sat there a while, wanting to allow the woman privacy for her grief, but needing to return to the church before I had to return the key. I wondered why the caretaker had not warned me that someone else had borrowed a key and might need some private time.

While I waited, I rewrote my scribbled notes. Through the rear view mirror I saw the door from the church open. Through it stepped the woman. In the shadow of the dark doorway she was being consoled by a tall man. With his arm around her shoulder, he led her to the back of the church. I knew a path wound through the woods back there, towards the large house where the general's descendants still lived.

In the brief moments before the couple disappeared round the corner and into the trees, I got the impression of a long dress beneath a black bonnet. The man seemed to be wearing a tweed suit of a different style. But the rear window was running with rivulets of rain and my glimpse was fleeting.

I returned to the church, completed my research, then closed it up and left.

As instructed, I placed the key in a hiding place at the caretaker's house. Later, I phoned to make sure he had found it. I told him of the lady who had been grieving, and of the man I hadn't seen inside the church, but who had escorted her as she left.

There was a long silence on the other end of the phone. And then, "You're the only person who has borrowed a key today." Another pause before, "Perhaps you saw the general?"

This time, the silence was at my end of the phone. It was broken when the caretaker spoke again, somewhat nervously. "They say that he felt for all those who lost children, and whenever he could, he'd visit the parents to help them. He lost his own daughter when she was only 16. He felt responsible for so many he'd brought here, so far from home."

He continued, "You're not the first to hear and see that mother crying. And nobody will walk that path between the church and the big house after dark. Years ago people used to talk about the Church Path ghosts."

Again, I didn't know what to say.

"I could have warned you," he continued. "But then you probably wouldn't have believed me. And the chances are you wouldn't have seen anything anyway. I hope you understand."

I told him that I did, and that, up until that day, I had never believed in ghosts. I'm still trying to think of a logical explanation for what I saw and heard that stormy, early evening in October. I don't think there is one.

A few days later, we took the Grade Four students to the church and graveyard. It was a bright and sunny fall morning. Not a day for ghosts.

But I did make sure I was first one into the church that day, just in case.

~~~***~~~

The Ghost Truck of Russiantown

Janet McGinity

On a crisp late-October day, two men in orange vests parked their pickup truck on the gravel shoulder of a road in rural Albert County, across the Petitcodiac River from Moncton. The two men dropped the truck's back gate and drew out gun cases holding .30-30 rifles plus extra ammunition. Two large rucksacks carried their water bottles and food for the day.

Jack and Fred Sinclair weren't familiar with the area. Usually, the brothers hunted near the Bay of Fundy coast, looking for deer-yards, tree-encircled fields where the white-tails gathered for shelter and food in late fall. But this year, they'd had no luck in their usual spots.

Bob McKinley, an acquaintance, had suggested an area called the Russiantown Road.

"You walk in about a mile on an old lane off the Mitton Road," Bob told them. "It should still be visible. Talk to George Geldart at the general store in Elgin; he knows where it is."

On their way, the Sinclairs stopped at the store to consult George.

"Where you going, boys? The Russiantown Road? Sure, I know where that is," he said. "Used to be a settlement in there, on a stream called the Calamingo. We don't know much about the people who lived there. They stuck together, only came into the village for supplies. Folks heard they were having a hard time, and then after a while, nobody saw them anymore. They say these people came from Russia, that's why the road was called the Russiantown Road."

George's father had once checked out a piece of land for sale up the Russiantown Road, but decided against it.

"Dad saw or heard something weird back there," he continued. "He said it was a place best left alone. That was years ago. I haven't heard of anyone going in for a long time—60, 70 years. If there are any deer, they won't be skittish. Good hunting to you, boys. Drop by later and let me know how you made out."

A hazy sun shone weakly through thin clouds as the Sinclairs got their hunting gear ready for the trek into Russiantown. White birch, beech, and pasture spruce lined the roadside and the abandoned meadow beyond. A ragged opening was visible where the tree cover thinned out. Overhead, a Northern Harrier soared in loose circles, watching for the tiniest movement of mice and voles in the dried meadow-grass. Other than the papery rustle of beech leaves, it was silent.

"Let's hope we find some good hunting here," grunted Jack, as he shouldered the gun case and slammed the truck gate closed. "What I wouldn't give to bag an eight- or 10-point buck! That'd be enough to keep a family in venison for months."

"Looks like decent country for deer," Fred answered. "Woods aren't too thick. Deer get around better where there's a mix of open and wooded areas. At least we might have better luck than we did by the coast—that was three days of tromping for nothing."

The brothers cradled their rifles in their arms and lifted the rucksacks over their shoulders. Crunching over dead leaves, they started along the lane and passed into thicker woods. The ground gradually rose as they tramped. Grasses grew knee-deep along the lane, which was little more than a wide space between the birches and young maples.

After half an hour's walk, Fred and Jack came to a shallow, rocky stream where the lane ended. Hoof marks pocked the wet mud near the water's edge, a sign that deer were drinking there.

"This must be the Calamingo Stream," Jack said. "Looks like that's where we are, according to the topo map. Let's take a look around."

The brothers pushed their way through knee-high grasses. The stream narrowed, and then meandered in an oxbow curve. That shallow area was the obvious crossing point for a bridge or a ford. The water was only a few inches deep. A level plateau was visible on the far side of the stream. They sloshed through the shallow water.

On the plateau, about 20 fallen-in cellar holes gaped where houses once stood. Bits of weathered timbers, long-rusted metal and raspberry canes filled the holes. Lilacs and rhubarb gone to seed straggled along the edges. The brothers poked through stone rubble, finding broken glass from an old canning jar, pieces of china, and a twisted fork.

It was very quiet. The brothers found themselves looking nervously over their shoulders. Even the air seemed hushed, as if it was holding its breath.

"I wonder what happened to them," mused Fred. "Who were these people anyway? Why did they abandon the place? Where did they go?"

A sudden, harsh cry cut the silence. Overhead, the harrier hurtled to the ground, and swooped upwards with a meadow-vole grasped in its curved talons.

"What the heck is that?" Jack pointed.

Piles of rock lay at intervals on the plateau. There must have been 50 of them. Each was about two feet high, five or six feet long, and rounded on top like a whale's back. Curious, the brothers moved in for a closer look. Fred spied something on top of one of the larger piles. It was a pair of white birch branches, tied in a rough cross shape with a piece of twine. Beneath it appeared the dull glint of metal.

He brushed away bits of loose birch bark to reveal a twisted picture frame, containing a tintype of a seated, unsmiling woman in a headscarf and full-skirted dress. In her arms, she held a tightly wrapped baby. Beside her stood a tall, thin man with a bushy moustache, wearing an ill-fitting suit. Fred handed the picture to Jack, who shook his head slowly. They looked around at the symmetrical rows of rock piles.

The hard noon-day sun beat down on the silent field. Water pattered in the nearly-dry stream. A thin breeze rustled dead leaves on the white birch trees. Fred scratched his head under the hunter-orange cap and grunted. He replaced the picture frame.

"I think it's time for lunch," he said. "Let's find a spot to eat. This place gives me the willies."

The two brothers followed the stream a short way to the lane. They found two large smooth boulders with flat tops, which would do for a lunch table.

Each man took a sandwich from a waxed paper package and opened a thermos. The crackle of the paper seemed unnaturally loud. After their lunch, Jack lit a pipe and lay back on the boulder, puffing. Fred sipped his tea and meditatively watched clouds drift past.

A shimmer appeared in the air, like heat haze on a hot summer day, but this was October. Off to their left came a faint rumbling noise, like a stone rolling on rough ground. Puzzled, the brothers sat up on the boulders, ears cocked.

"Did you hear that?"

They looked at each other. "Must have been the wind."

The rumbling grew louder. They stared, but the road was empty. Something was approaching. In the still air, they heard the chugga-chugga-chugga of an old engine. The invisible vehicle clattered along the bumpy lane. About 20 feet away from them, the engine sound stopped. They heard the sound of a door opening, a squeak of hinges needing oil, footsteps crunching on gravel, a heavy *whump*, and then another *whump*. Again they heard the sound of a door opening and closing with a bang. The chugga-chugga-chugga noise started again, at first loud, then faded as it moved away from them.

Fred and Jack looked at each other in consternation, then stepped off the boulder and walked to where they had heard the noises. There were no tire marks in the damp earth.

"What on earth was that?" Jack said. "There's nobody but us for miles. But I sure as hell heard an old car or a truck."

The light breeze died down, and the air felt suddenly oppressive. The weird sounds, the birch cross, a metal-framed picture, and piles of rock along the stream... something was very wrong. Even the wind seemed to whisper, *leave... leave... leave.*

Fred and Jack hurriedly picked up their belongings and found their way back to the stream and the half-grown lane into Russiantown. It took them an hour to walk to their truck. They drove back to the Elgin store.

Pickup trucks lined the front of it. A white sign in the window advertised hunting and fishing licenses for sale. Inside, the store carried everything rural folk needed: cold glass bottles of cola in a red metal cooler, hardware, rubber boots, sturdy clothing, tools, ammunition, a few limp vegetables, and fruit in a fogged refrigerator cabinet.

"We did make it to Russiantown," Jack announced to George, who was putting two icy cold colas on the counter. "Didn't find any deer," he said. "But we were glad to get the hell out of there. Kind of a creepy spot."

George pondered a moment, and wiped his hands across the knee of his overalls.

"Why'd you find it creepy?" he asked. "Did you see something?"

"Yes, we did," answered Jack. "But the strangest things were the sounds."

He recounted what they'd heard, the sound of the old car or truck, and the rock piles near the stream. By then, several older men had gathered around the store counter, curious to hear the conversation.

"What happened out there?" asked Jack.

George's face crinkled, and he shook his head.

"Wiped out," he muttered. "They were wiped out, the whole damn lot of them."

He remembered his father talking of a group of Russian-speaking immigrants who'd arrived to claim the land they'd been granted in the late 1800s. Most of them spoke no English, and they practiced an unfamiliar religion. The Russians worked long, back-breaking days to wring a living from the soil.

For two generations, the settlers survived, but didn't mingle much with Albert County folk. Memories of the persecution they had suffered in the Old Country were still fresh, and they did not want to draw attention to themselves. Money was scarce. During several particularly harsh winters, they had barely enough food to keep them alive.

Then one spring day, a little girl got sick with a virulent disease. She lasted only a few weeks before her face turned blue as she gasped for breath. She died suddenly. No one knew what the strange disease was. Next to go was the little girl's older brother.

The parents, overcome with grief, tried to dig graves for them, but hit bedrock only a foot down. They decided that at least they could build cairns to mark the children's resting place. One of the villagers, who spoke a little English, was delegated to travel to the village of Petitcodiac to order coffins from the local undertaker. Thus were placed the first two small rock piles in the field along the Calamingo stream.

Over the course of a year, the mysterious illness raged through the small community. The arrival of the undertaker in his Model T pickup truck delivering more coffins became a weekly occurrence.

Word seeped out around the county about the illness. The locals wanted to help, but feared they might catch this disease which felled entire families in a few months. Even the undertaker was uneasy. Finally, he stopped driving down the road into the community. He went as far only as the river, stopped the truck, opened the door and dropped the coffins onto the ground, where they landed with a *whump*.

The number of rock piles grew. Finally, the last few Russiantown settlers abandoned the little community and travelled to western Canada, where other Russians lived. Such sorrow could not be borne.

"People didn't want to go into the settlement, even after the last of them left," said George. "Nobody knew where this sickness came from. They were afraid that maybe the water was bad, or that the Russiantown folks had an inherited a disease from the Old Country."

He looked at the two hunters.

"You fellas are the first to go into what used to be Russiantown for a very long time."

He paused.

"Dad went back there by himself. He told us later he'd heard an old truck coming by, and then a *whump*, like something wooden hitting rocky ground. But he only heard the one. I wonder why you heard two."

The little group around the store counter fell silent. The two hunters gathered their cold drinks, and paid for them. They walked to their truck and drove away, past the abandoned road leading to a woods clearing with empty cellar-holes, lonely rock cairns, and a ghost truck.

~~~***~~~

Changes

Diane Losier

Gillian breathed a deep sigh of relief as she lay face down on the narrow massage table. She gratefully let herself sink under the expert hands of her masseuse, Sarah, as she kneaded a knot on her tense back muscles. Gillian practically ran to these weekly visits. The stress of being an elementary school teacher was really getting to her lately. Was she becoming less patient or were the students more difficult to deal with? She didn't remember it always being this way; the sense of entitlement, the constant need to be entertained, or problems accepting responsibility. *I can't keep this up much longer*, she thought. She tried to relax and focus on the soothing music while Sarah's fingers massaged a particularly hard knot between her shoulder blades.

The weather was miserable. After a few glorious sunny days, February's weather, now at its worst, poured sheets of heavy rain against her windshield. It took Gillian 30 minutes to drive home from Halifax. Fanny Fluff met her at the door expecting to be fed as usual. There was no one else to greet her these days. Her daughter, Mary Ellen, lived in France with her husband, and Gillian was divorced, so there was no spouse to contend with at home.

Gillian had no energy after the divorce to engage in a new relationship. "Too complicated! Been there, done that!" She sometimes told Fanny Fluff that her quiet little ways were all she could handle right now. Lately however, her solitude seeped into her consciousness. She kept a daily journal, which was like a drug for her, keeping at bay the reality of her deep discontent.

Gillian barely got through the last few weeks of school. It was her physician, Dr. Barton, who advised her to take a medical leave of absence. She considered his advice and decided to go away for March Break.

Cuba was heaven! Her body relaxed under the relentless hot sun, but not her mind. She confided nightly in her journal and each morning she recorded her dreams. Although she was in a warm paradise, her dreams were all about cold and snow.

3:15 a.m., March 18
Weird dream. I'm with people. Don't know who. Against everyone's advice, I set off to cross-country ski into a vast white wilderness. I know it's dangerous but feel compelled to keep going. After a while, I turn and look at where I came from. The wind blew away all traces of where I've been. I'm lost and I don't care. Then I notice a pulsating silver light and head back toward it, oblivious of the uncertainties that lie beyond.

The dream woke Gillian up as dawn broke. It was the catalyst she needed to stop teaching for a while, to step out of her comfort zone and leave herself open to new possibilities.

Coming home from the all-inclusive resort was a rude awakening. She had to inform her principal, Mr. Wallis, of her decision, complete the paper work, and face the anxiety of having nothing in particular to do with her days. Dr. Barton recommended Prozac. However, Gillian deeply distrusted any medication and decided to make a go of it on her own. She knew she needed to keep busy, but she felt she needed a different kind of busyness, something to nourish her battered soul. She settled on a daily routine of meditation and yoga and enrolled in a creative writing class. Gillian enjoyed her new lifestyle so much that after a few weeks, she decided to quit teaching altogether. She had put in 25 years, enough for a modest pension. Plus she had that nest-egg from her mother's estate waiting for a "rainy day". Well, this was it!

Gillian slept fitfully. She had finally decided to quit her job. Now she was considering selling her house and moving to the country. She kept tossing and turning, caught between a life she no longer wanted and the unknown. The uncertainties kept her stomach in a knot until she finally fell asleep just before dawn.

Sunday morning dawned cloudy and cold. Her nightly worries continued to weigh heavily on her shoulders. She reached for her journal. It was a large sketchbook, big enough for her bold handwriting and thick enough to last a year. She called it her cheap therapist as she often got as much clarity from an hour of writing as she did from an expensive session with her psychologist. By the time she had noted the pros and cons of these new undertakings, she was convinced that it was a good idea.

In early May, nature was transforming and blossoming, and so was Gillian. She still struggled with the idea of selling her house, but it felt like the right time and the right choice.

Two weeks after putting the sign on her lawn, she drove to the Annapolis Valley. Life untangled itself on that glorious morning into a single stream of sheer happiness. Now that the tough decisions had been made, she felt exhilarated by the freedom and promise of new adventures. She surfed the Web daily for a country house but nothing jumped out at her, so she drove around and followed her nose, letting chance have a part in her future for a change.

The Annapolis Valley in spring was a veritable fairy tale. Gillian loved driving along the winding country roads, marvelling at the beauty of the apple orchards in full bloom. She remembered after-school picnics with Mary Ellen under ancient apple trees, their arching branches covered with thousands of fragrant white blossoms. They would lie back on the blanket and gaze contentedly at the wide expanse of blue on blue; deep blue sky over the deeper blue of the ocean below. Occasionally, they were lulled to sleep by the drone of hundreds of honey bees busily collecting pollen as they flew from blossom to blossom.

She noticed the tide was out. The Fundy tides were the highest in the world, with the water levels changing by more than seven metres twice daily. Once, she had walked out on the muddy ocean floor at night, with millions of stars both shining from above and reflecting from below on the wet sand. It had felt like walking in outer space!

After a sharp turn and a dip in the road, Gillian came upon her favourite little harbour. Usually, three or four brightly coloured fishing boats would either be bobbing on the swiftly incoming tide or, like this morning, leaning on their sides. This was the road to Blomidon, the red clay headland made famous in Nova Scotia Mi'kmaq legends as the home of Glooscap, the creator of the Universe.

On her way back from Blomidon, Gillian explored a side road she hadn't noticed before. She turned right and slowed down to enjoy the drive along the narrow winding road. At a bend in the road, she suddenly noticed a large Remax FOR SALE sign hidden in the brambles. She slowed to a stop, backed up, and turned right down a narrow driveway winding down to a small glen. There it was, her house! Gillian knew the instant she saw it.

A line of hemlocks shaded the driveway down to the two-storey white house. A majestic maple tree towered over the front veranda. To the north of the house, a stand of birch trees swayed in the breeze. Gillian quickly stepped out of her car to examine the place more closely. She noticed a pale figure standing at one of the upstairs windows. Was someone home? Gillian waved but as she approached the house, the figure vanished.

Upon closer inspection, she discovered the house was obviously deserted. The porch was half rotted; the roof and windows needed to be replaced. However, the foundation looked solid and the wood siding was in good shape. To her delight, she discovered a narrow path at the back that led through raspberry bushes down to a shallow babbling river.

Gillian hardly contained her excitement as she dialled the realtor's number on her cell phone.

"Ted Garrett here," replied a friendly voice.

"Hello, Mr. Garrett. My name is Gillian Fleming from Halifax. I was driving around this afternoon and saw your sign in front of the two-storey white house on route 221. Is it still for sale?"

Mr. Garrett's voice brightened as he replied, "Why yes! That's the old MacLeod farm."

"I apologize for calling after business hours but would it be possible to see the house before I return to Halifax?"

"I don't see why not! It's always business hours when you're a real-estate agent! I can meet you at the house right after supper, say 6:30?"

"That's great! See you then."

Mr. Garrett met her in front of the house as scheduled. The front door creaked as it opened on its rusty hinges. The downstairs rooms were small and dusty but Gillian noticed the gentle beauty of the warm evening sun pouring through the living room windows. A large kitchen was in the back with a view of the river valley. There was a bathroom upstairs along with two bedrooms. The larger bedroom overlooked the maple tree at the front of the house. She imagined herself sitting at a desk in the alcove where she would gaze at the line of hemlocks swaying in the wind.

By the time they left the property, the sun had dropped behind the clouds and it was getting chilly. As they drove off, they didn't see the old lace curtain in the left dormer window slowly rise and fall.

Someone has finally come....

On Monday morning, after a weekend of comparing prices and other properties, she called Mr. Garrett.

"How much are they asking for the property?"

"They're asking $35,000," he replied.

"That's a bit low for a property with river frontage. Is there something you're not telling me?"

Gillian thought she heard a moment of hesitation in Mr. Garrett's voice. "Well, this is the country, don't forget, not like the inflated city real-estate market. As far as I know, the house is sound. Nothing that a few repairs and a fresh coat of paint won't fix. To tell you the truth, people find the house too small. Plus, that house has been on the market for a few years now and that doesn't help either."

The agent was beginning to sound a bit too eager and Gillian wondered if this was a good idea after all.

"Thanks for all this information Mr. Garrett. I think I'll hire a house inspector and get back to you," replied Gillian.

"No problem! Call me anytime!"

By the end of the week the house inspector assured her that the house was basically sound.

The following Monday, Gillian e-mailed Mr. Garrett and put in a ridiculously low counter-offer which, to her amazement, was accepted. She never met the owners; all business was carried out through a lawyer in Port Williams. Meanwhile, she received a decent offer on her city house, which she saw as a very good sign. "When you're on the right path, the Universe helps you along." She had read that somewhere.

It was mid-June by the time all the documentation for both houses was complete. The first thing she did was hire a contractor to redo the roof of her new house, rebuild the veranda, and replace all the windows. Then she spent days sorting through the things she had held on to since Mary Ellen was a baby. When moving day came, two of her friends, Melanie and Donna, offered to spend their weekend helping her settle in. By Sunday evening, they were sitting on her new veranda at sunset, sharing a huge pizza and beer.

Later that night, Gillian took her cat on a tour of the house. When they came to the small bedroom, she was surprised when Fanny snarled and jumped out of her arms into the hallway.

The weeks after moving in flew by. In spite of having no immediate neighbours, Gillian didn't feel lonely. She sometimes stopped to chat with Joanne, the local post mistress, or with the cheery young woman at the local diner. Everyone was friendly and curious about her situation, wondering why she had moved there and how she was getting along at the old MacLeod place. In fact, after a while, it irked her to be constantly asked how she was getting along. She was perfectly capable of running a house on her own!

Still, it did occur to her that she might be vulnerable. She found an animal shelter in Wolfville, the university town five kilometres from her new home. What a heart-breaking experience! Some dogs ran up and licked her fingers while others huddled in the back of their cages, too scared or indifferent to bother. A lab-shepherd mix caught Gillian's eye the first time she walked around the compound. At first, the mid-sized female stayed back but on the second turn she approached and poked her nose through the wire cage. She looked up with sad eyes and a sorrowful whine. Gillian decided to call her Maggie.

The following day, after all the formalities were done, Gillian drove home wondering how Maggie would get along with Fanny Fluff. Maggie dashed into the house, sniffing everywhere, and as soon as the cat saw this big animal, she scrambled upstairs. Gillian knew she'd find her hiding under her bed. Fanny Fluff never went into the small bedroom. In spite of this unpromising start, Gillian was confident the two animals would eventually settle into a peaceful co-existence.

By the end of July, the field near the house was covered with brown-eyed Susans. Gillian chose a few colours for the upstairs area and painted her bedroom. That night she slept in the other bedroom as the paint in her own room hadn't dried. The smaller bedroom still had the blue and white wallpaper from ages ago, yellowing and peeling in some places. In spite of the balmy weather, it felt damp and draughty. She pulled out an extra blanket and settled in bed with her current book. She must have fallen asleep while reading. Hours later, she awoke with a start. The glow from the bare light bulb broke into the shattered pieces of her dream. She reached out for her journal.

2:15 a.m., July 12
Another weird dream. Lying face-up on a hard surface in complete darkness. No fear just sharp awareness. Felt this presence floating over me, its face inches from mine. Overwhelming sadness. Started sobbing deep inside myself. Woke up. What is this?

Gillian couldn't stay in that room another minute. She felt a presence following her, breathing with her, observing her. She was wide awake now, so she went downstairs to make herself a cup of herbal tea and curled up on the sofa to await the dawn. She was soon jolted out of a fitful sleep by Fanny Fluff jumping on her chest and purring loudly, demanding her breakfast. Gillian spent the morning putting furniture back into her bedroom. She had planned to paint the blue bedroom but after her nightmare, she was reluctant to enter it. She decided to install some wainscoting in the bathroom and paint the other rooms instead.

When she tired of working on the house, Gillian explored the area, often biking along the flat country roads that ran parallel to North Mountain.

By mid-August the house was almost done. She should have felt deeply satisfied. Instead she was feeling restless.

8 a.m., Aug. 23
Something's wrong. Where has all my energy gone? I guess I should expect a slump after all those changes. The constant drizzle this past week isn't helping. I'm really noticing how alone I am. The weird thing is, I wake up each morning with a feeling of foreboding. I'm trying to remember my dreams but all I feel is that I've been in a dark place. Most mornings I wake up feeling chilly, with a knot in my stomach. Maybe I was too hasty in making such a drastic move to the country. I should have just taken a leave of absence and stayed in my house for a while. If this constant rain would finally let up, I could get out, go biking, do something.

The unusually cold, damp weather continued. Her daily walks with Maggie helped a bit.

She tried to be out of the house as often as possible, often going to the local coffee shop for breakfast in the hopes of alleviating this growing feeling of unease. It was the evenings she particularly dreaded.

125

She didn't watch much television so she filled her evenings with DVD movies and surfing the Net. Invariably, she fell asleep as soon as it became dark, only to sleep fitfully, not remembering much of what she dreamt. She often went downstairs in the middle of the night to sleep on the couch, hoping the change would help settle her. She felt she needed to visit her therapist or, at the very least, get some sleeping pills.

By now she was looking forward to her friend's visit. Donna said she couldn't make it but Melanie confirmed for the Labour Day weekend. Gillian was overjoyed to see her again. Although Melanie was a petite brunette, she had the energy of 10 people.

"I love the country feel of this place," said Melanie. "How old is the house?"

"I was told it was built around 1940," answered Gillian. "The previous owners redid the cedar shingles."

"Maybe we can find a few antiques in Annapolis Royal," called Melanie as she headed downstairs.

In no time, both women were sipping wine and cooking up a storm while singing along to "The Country and Western Show" on the local radio station. What a relief to finally have laughter in her house!

That night, Melanie refused Gillian's offer to sleep in her room. Instead, she settled herself in the blue bedroom. Gillian hadn't confided any of her misgivings to her friend as she still wasn't sure what was going on. She fell asleep wondering if Melanie would sleep well. She hoped this would settle whether something was really happening or if she was actually starting to lose it.

As it turned out, Melanie was a very light sleeper and had the habit of sleeping while listening to sounds of nature on her MP3 player. The music was still on when she woke the next morning. She felt rested but wondered why she was so chilly; it was a warm summer day.

"How did you sleep?" asked Gillian at breakfast.

"I slept like a log," replied Melanie. "I was wondering what you'll do with Fanny and Maggie while we're gone?"

"Oh, I've arranged to board Maggie at a kennel and Fanny Fluff can manage on her own for a couple of days."

"Any plans for our trip tomorrow?"

"Well, I thought we'd have lunch at a cute Austrian cafe on the waterfront. Their pastry is to die for! Then we could visit 'The

Habitation'. It's the site of Champlain's second French settlement in Canada."

"Sounds great!" replied Melanie.

Their weekend visit was all too brief. The two women shared long walks and wonderful meals accompanied by non-stop talking and laughter. Gillian found a set of antique dishes in one of the quaint shops. Later that evening, Melanie surprised her with a beautiful old pitcher.

"For those wonderful wild flowers," she said. "Thank you for a great weekend!"

"No, thank *you* for all the help," replied Gillian.

They returned on Labour Day and picked up Maggie at the kennel before going to the house. Fanny Fluff was anxiously waiting at the front door, happy to have them back.

Gillian hadn't felt so good in weeks. A weight had lifted along with the bad weather. Re-energized, she decided to finally paint the small bedroom. She boldly decided to sleep in the blue room and put to rest the uneasiness that had grown over the past few weeks. After all, Melanie had slept very well in that room!

The air still felt unusually chilly. However, Gillian, determined to prove her fears groundless, simply pulled out a blanket from the bottom drawer of the bureau. She quickly fell into an exhausted sleep.

The hours passed. Unseen, a bank of dark stormy clouds slowly covered the bright starry sky. Maggie was sleeping curled up on the rug in Gillian's room. Fanny Fluff had cautiously crept into the blue room and was blissfully asleep near Gillian's head. Suddenly, Fanny was wide awake. The fur on the back of her neck rose as she anxiously peered into the darkness. Her eyes scanned the shadowy room and a slow growl rose from deep in her throat.

Gillian was enjoying a dreamless sleep. Suddenly, she awoke. She was no longer in the small bedroom but in a completely black space. She couldn't move. She felt suspended in a darkness so thick it was almost a physical presence. The total absence of light gradually sucked the air from around her and she began to gasp for breath. She woke up in a cold sweat. This time she was truly awake.

She tried to turn on the bedside lamp but it wouldn't work. She heard the howling wind and rain outside her window and figured there was a power outage. Trembling with fear, she pulled the top blanket around her shoulders and felt her way to the bathroom where she kept an emergency flashlight on the counter. She flicked on the light and to her horror there was another face, a young woman's face, superimposed over her own pale reflection. The young woman's long bushy hair formed an ashen halo around her head, white tendrils floating into the surrounding darkness.

"Oh my God!" shrieked Gillian. She tore off the blanket and hurtled down the stairs. She quickly found her raincoat and boots, grabbed her keys, and was out of the house in a flash.

Mercifully, the car started on the first turn. As she sped down the narrow country road toward Wolfville, she was shaking so hard she could hardly keep the car on the road. "Oh my God! Oh My God!" she kept repeating as she sped into the inky darkness. Her headlights picked out the looming silhouettes of blowing trees and the darker hulks of farmhouses and barns. She sobbed with relief when she saw a tiny line of street lights shining in the distance. The houses were all dark, even the service station was closed. Gillian headed for Tim Horton's which she knew was open all night long.

The two women behind the counter were astonished to see someone arrive at 2 a.m. in the middle of the worst storm of the summer. Surprise gave way to alarm when they noticed Gillian's dishevelled appearance, her wild eyes, and her wet pyjama legs dripping onto the floor.

"Good Lord!" cried the older woman. "What's going on? Are you all right, dear?"

Gillian slumped in a chair and wept. It took her a few minutes to calm down. In bits and pieces she told the two concerned women about the draughty room, the dreams, and the vision in the mirror. The women exchanged knowing glances.

"Well dear, no one wanted to say so before. Didn't want to scare you in case nothing happened, but that house was empty for a reason. You see, 20 years ago there was a family living there. They had a teenage daughter. Nice folks. Well, one day the couple came back from the movies to find the house empty. At first they thought their daughter had biked to a friend's house. By midnight, they started phoning around. The girl never came back. It was the talk of the town for months. The police found absolutely no clues. The TV was still on, a snack half eaten on the coffee table. What a sin! The parents moved away of course...."

"It must be her ghost haunting my house," sniffled Gillian. "Maybe she's trying to tell me something. I can't take any more of this!"

The next day, Gillian moved out. She stayed in the city for a while with Melanie, trying to decide what to do next. What a mess! She'd retired, sold her home, and now her new house probably wouldn't sell with a story like that going around! She tried to fill her days as best she could but she was worried sick. She decided to put the house up for sale. What else could she do?

After a few weeks, she moved into a furnished apartment and tried to get her life back in order. By early November, no one had showed any interest in the house. She decided it was time to clear her things out. Once again, Melanie offered to help.

They drove to Port Williams on a Friday evening and stayed at the local B&B. By Sunday afternoon most of the packing was done and Melanie went to town to get a pizza. Gillian decided to take Maggie for a walk following a path along the river. It was a grey day with the promise of snow in the air. Gillian walked briskly, her hands deep in her pockets, the events of the past few months going round and round in her mind.

It took a while to notice that Maggie was gone. Gillian whistled for her. Presently, Maggie came bounding out of the woods but soon disappeared in the underbrush. *That darn dog*, she thought, making her way into the dense bushes. She once again heard Maggie come crashing through the undergrowth. Gillian finally spotted her dog peeking at her from behind a stand of small spruce trees. She seemed to have something in her mouth but darted back into the forest before Gillian could reach her. This time, Gillian kept up with her until they came to a small clearing. Maggie was furiously digging into a pile of fallen leaves. Gillian quickly came up intending to grab her collar. What she saw, though, made her recoil in horror.

Lying by Maggie's head was what appeared to be a human bone, a femur maybe. The dog kept on digging, trying to get to the rest of his find. Gillian had no doubt as to what Maggie had found. It had to be the body of that poor girl. She grabbed Maggie by the collar, snapped on her leash and dragged her back along the path as fast as she could run.

Melanie was already back with the pizza. Gillian burst into the house, her eyes wild with horror. They immediately called 911.

Gillian's story was pretty straightforward. The police officer noted her information and told her they would call as soon as they had some news. After they left, the two women returned to the B&B. Gillian took a sleeping pill and was out for the night.

A week later, Gillian got the call. The DNA evidence matched. It was the body of the missing girl. The officer informed Gillian that the girl's parents had been informed. They were in shock but extremely grateful to Gillian for having finally brought them some closure.

After the great upheaval of the past few months, Gillian was once again back in the city. She and Melanie had moved her boxes of personal belongings but had left the furniture behind. There was no question of going back for a while. She decided to put all that behind her and concentrate on the present, one day at a time.

Another Christmas came and went, another long cold winter. This time Gillian went to a different resort. By spring, she felt she had enough courage to return to the country and finally move her furniture. Melanie wasn't available but Donna offered to help.

They drove to the country house on Saturday morning, taking Fanny Fluff with them. Her brother, who was staying in her apartment for the weekend, was allergic to cats. By afternoon they decided to go to Wolfville for a coffee break. Gillian had already told Donna all the details of her ordeal. They speculated about what exactly happened that fateful night so long ago.

They were about to cross the street when a sudden gust of wind blew Gillian's hat to the ground behind her. As she stepped back to retrieve it, a low sports car careened through the crosswalk, barely missing the people coming the other way. Had Gillian not reached back for her hat she would have been hit! She stood there, hat in hand, staring at the car which was rapidly receding in the distance. As she turned back to speak to Donna, she saw her reflection in the large display window behind her. To her astonishment, she distinctly saw a white shadow swirl around her and, quickly rising, disappear in the sky. Her heart sank! What if her ordeal wasn't over?

Gillian was quiet on the way home. She didn't tell Donna about what she had seen. When they got back to the house, though, it felt different somehow. The chill was gone and she found Fanny Fluff asleep in the blue bedroom. Donna was surprised when Gillian suggested they stay overnight, given all that she had heard. Gillian finally told Donna about the vision in the store window, and understood why she wanted to stay overnight. Maybe this whole nightmare was finally coming to a close.

It took Gillian a long time to fall asleep in the blue bedroom. She was comforted by the presence of Fanny Fluff curled up in the crook of her legs. Just before dawn, she fell into a deep, dreamless sleep. When she awoke an hour later, chickadees were chirping merrily outside the open window. Gillian stretched out lazily, breathing in the rich aroma of coffee brewing in the kitchen. She slipped on her robe, and slowly made her way down the stairs.

"What's for breakfast?" she asked.

~~~***~~~

My Booots!
Tom Robson

When we moved to Nova Scotia in 1979, I met a ghost.

My first 35 years had been spent in England where, if you believe half the stories you were told, every second dwelling is infested with ghosts. But I was one of life's skeptics. I never saw or heard of an apparition that couldn't be explained away. I simply did not believe in ghosts.

I lived many of my English years close to the ocean. I liked having access to salt water and shorelines. After living for seven years in or near Montreal, my wife and I decided to move. I wanted to return to the ocean. Our dream was to become part of a small community beside the sea. Ideally, we would find oceanfront property somewhere in the Maritimes.

There was the problem of finding jobs to replace those which we knew were soon to vanish. We had some Maritime contacts so, as soon as our summer vacation commenced, we threw camping equipment into the car and headed east to explore job opportunities.

Way out on the Eastern shore, within a rural community, I accepted a teaching job. The same afternoon, we found our dream home.

We had been driving around, looking and asking about available properties until we were seduced by a "For Sale" sign at the top of an overgrown driveway. We pushed through tangled alders, and burst upon a storey and a half house set against a backdrop of sunshine, with a sparkling summer sea fronting offshore islands. The opposite bank of the wide estuary shone spruce green on that glorious July day. The house was empty but phone enquiries led to a quickly arranged meeting with a bemused agent. We drove the 100 plus kilometres to Dartmouth. When we marched into her office the next morning, set to buy this long empty property, she must have thought it was Christmas in July. The next day, she followed us down east and showed us round the house and property, on which the sun was still shining. Though overgrown and somewhat faded and neglected, we were still entranced by the prospect of restoring and living in it.

We would be buying seven and a half acres of land, with 500 feet of ocean frontage, set on the fringe of a community where I was to work. Surely, we could gain acceptance and then become integral components of that town.

We were novices in the world of Nova Scotia real estate. The entire transaction took only 10 days. Good deals never happened this fast and easy. We overlooked basic safeguards such as having the property independently inspected. We simply thought we had hit the jackpot. We convinced ourselves that any work that needed doing to make the house habitable and comfortable could be done after we moved in. We'd find any money needed as easily as the real estate agent had found us a mortgage for this "gem".

Three weeks later, with our belongings following in the moving van a couple of days behind us, we hot footed it back from Montreal, to our idyll.

It was raining and the wind was blowing onshore when we saw it again. The faded, black painted house, with grass, alders, weeds and bushes threatening to consume it, was less inviting. Inside, the wind whistled through the shingled walls and rattled the doors and windows.

We had two days to find the necessary tradesmen to get the well water flowing and electricity functioning. My real job didn't start for more than a month. We naively assumed that would give us ample time to make our 100-year-old dream house comfortable.

For the two nights before our belongings arrived, we decided to camp out on the floor of our new-to-us house. That first night we snuggled in our sleeping bags in the living room, safe from a summer storm, dreaming our delusions and planning to resurrect our estate.

With all our ever-changing schemes, and the growing list of problems playing on our mind, sleep was impossible.

My wife and I bedded down on the pine planked floor of the dark and isolated house. Its silence contrasted to the city sounds and lights outside our former Montreal apartment window, with which we were so familiar.

Few lights worked in this gloomy, distressed house. There were no outside lights. The infrequent traffic noise and passing headlights were muffled by the 100 metres of scrub between us and the road. We even heard the waves break on the shingle shore 50 metres in the other direction. The diminishing wind still seemed to find cracks and crannies, through which it whistled into and under the house.

And then there were rustling noises and scratching sounds that disturbed the wind-whistle isolation. The house had been empty for two years. Other than a crawl space where the well pump and furnace were housed, the post and beam building rested on a beach stone foundation from which many stones were absent. Who knew what wildlife was under our floor, in the walls, or under our roof?

The new problem of identifying noises was more fodder to stimulate our tired but overactive minds. Eventually, exhaustion defeated my meandering thoughts and I slept.

I was awakened from a deep, but too brief sleep, by frantic whispers from my wife, her mouth mere inches from my ear. My surprised, awakening grunt was quieted by the urgency of Barb's, "Ssshhhh!" and her hand covering my mouth.

"There's somebody upstairs! Listen!" she whispered.

She was right. There were shuffling footsteps over our head; they weren't from a stocking footed field mouse or squirrel. Someone—or something—was moving in the empty bedroom above.

My watch glowed 3:15. If someone was up there, they must have known that we were in the house. Our car was parked feet from the back door.

"What do we do?" asked my wife, clinging to me, with fear in her stifled voice.

"I don't know!" I whispered back, clutching her tightly, as much for my reassurance as hers. "We'll wait to see what happens." That was my decisive plan of action.

Scarcely breathing, we waited. Even when the footsteps began to shuffle down the stairs, we waited. They turned down the hall towards us. The door from that hallway to the living room was already open. We were on the floor to the right of it, safely ensconced in our sleeping bags. I got ready to spring into action if our visitor turned towards us.

But, still in the pitch dark, our visitor turned right, into the kitchen, a 25-foot long add-on to the original storey and a half. As the footsteps shuffled the length of the kitchen, across the worn, linoleum floor, I thought I heard a male voice say just two words: "My booooooooots!"

"Boots" was drawn out into a long, plaintive enunciation, as though he was so emotionally attached to them that he was mourning their loss.

Then there was a metallic creak as a door opened, followed by a clanging noise.

Again: "My boooooots!"

At the far end of the kitchen was a door leading to the outside. It was closed, and we had no key for its lock. I'd been unable to move it earlier in the day. But, in the dark hours of that morning, we heard it open. And then it closed. The shuffling footsteps were no more.

Barb and I breathed again. We were still too scared to move, even though both our bladders beckoned us, most urgently, to go up those stairs to the bathroom.

I quietly scrambled for a flashlight that I'd laid somewhere near my pillow. "Don't turn it on yet!" urged Barb. "It may still be outside!"

"It?" I whispered. "Didn't you hear the voice? That was a man!"

"Sssshhhh!! Let's wait five minutes. Then you can check things out!" volunteered Barb. "What do you think that clanging noise was?" she asked. Her nervousness was making her more talkative than usual.

I'd already speculated that it was one of the doors on the very old wood stove and range that stood at the far end of the kitchen.

A while later, full bladders, insatiable curiosity, and a wife who wanted me as a super hero compelled me to turn on first the flashlight and then the few house lights that worked. The front, back, and the jammed door at the far end of the kitchen were all locked tight.

There was one open door. The wood stove had an oven door hinged at the bottom. The clanging and the metallic creak had been the result of that door being opened. I closed it. The door had been securely fastened with a latch. There was no way that it could've fallen open on its own.

There was a joint expedition to the bathroom where we flushed with water from a bucket, hauled earlier from the well. Both bedrooms were empty, as were the closets. There was nowhere for anybody to hide.

We didn't check the dark outside.

Back in our welcoming sleep spot, we lay there forever, speculating on what we'd heard. It was so country dark that we had seen nothing. But what were those sounds? Who had been in our house? How did he get in and out? Had he been hiding upstairs? What exactly had he said?

The questions were stilled as we snatched a little more sleep.

There were no answers for the mysterious noises when we woke to sunshine a few hours later. We searched the dilapidated shed and newer barns. We even checked the two-seater outhouse, a building we would probably have to employ until we could get water flowing from the well.

But there was much work to be done and many people to find before our belongings arrived the next day. Investigating our mysterious, wee-hours visitor was a low priority.

Of necessity, we met many new people that first full day in the community. Without exception, they identified us as the people who'd bought that house on the road to Temperance Island. It was variously identified as "the Crozier property", or "Mrs. O'T's house" or "The Strawberry Farm". The confused chronology and history of its previous owners was not clarified until late in the afternoon.

The local plumber, Frank, an elderly, garrulous fellow, arrived late afternoon to assess the well and pipes. After he'd checked the pump to see what parts were needed, he said he'd be back the next day but first suggested that we pour a jug of Javex down the well.

He was a keen conversationalist. When asked, he told us that the family that had long occupied the property was named Crozier. They had eventually sold it to a retired sea captain who grew strawberries there in the sixties. The last owner, Siobhan O'Toole, was a local teacher. She'd rented the place to people who had neglected and abused it before leaving. It had been empty for at least two winters.

He added, "You've got a load of work ahead of you here!"

We'd already come to that realization. We enquired about the age of the house.

"I don't know, but Isaac Crozier runs the local store. Ask him. He was born here so he should know," volunteered our friendly plumber.

"We thought someone was in here last night," Barb told him. "About three o'clock, we heard someone come down the stairs and go out the kitchen door."

Our talkative and knowledgeable plumber was, for the first time, silent. Eventually, he suggested we mention that event when we talked to Isaac at the store.

Before settling down on our hard, floorboard "bed" that second night, we thoroughly checked doors, windows and closets: upstairs and down. Earlier in the day, we'd even scrambled up into the uninsulated attic. Nothing there, either, except a primitive bootjack. Our first, sleepless night, followed by a hectic day, meant that we should sleep soundly, kept safe by the child's night light we'd bought. The only working power point where we could plug it in, though, was in the kitchen.

By 10:00 p.m. we were both sound asleep. I woke, with a start, to a voice whispering, "It's back!"

He was!

Again, he was shuffling down the stairs, though Barb had already heard him moving above our heads, as I snored. As before, he came towards our sleeping place, then turned away into the kitchen, moaning "My booooots!! My boooooots!!!!"

I sneaked a look past the door into the nightlight lit kitchen. I saw a man in a long sleeved shirt and coarse woolen pants tucked into his socks. He stopped at the stove and opened the oven door, which again creaked and clanked.

"My booooots!!!" he uttered. He turned, easily opened the jammed tight door on the ocean side of the house, and left.

Barb, too, had glimpsed this man, though neither of us could distinguish his features. "Was that a ghost?" she asked.

When I didn't respond, she added, insistently, "It must be!"

"Unless someone has a key to that door!" I replied; as always, I was looking for a logical explanation to discount a ghostly apparition.

The oven door was still down. The door through which our visitor had left was, again, jammed tight when we checked.

We lay there between 3:30 and 4:00 a.m., trying to make sense of the strange events of the successive nights. Barb was too scared to sleep. I racked my skeptical brain for the explanation that continued to escape me. Perhaps it was a ghost. Was it time to change my belief?

How could we find out about our "visitor"? Hopefully, Isaac, the corner store owner would have an explanation.

On waking, we again decided we had more pressing matters to deal with: urgent and practical situations for which we hoped we could find solutions.

For some time, we were preoccupied with the lengthy task of getting water to circulate through pipes that didn't leak. The house needed a thorough cleaning, too. Later in the day, our belongings had to be unloaded and sorted. We had also negotiated to have the house rewired once we learned that the old wiring was a fire hazard.

The ghost, if that's what our uninvited guest was, hid in the back of our minds once we began sleeping upstairs in our own bed, on that third night. He didn't appear. Or maybe he did, but he no longer disturbed us.

A few days later, on errands in the harbour, we had to stop at the store. I asked the man who served us if he was Mr. Crozier. He was, so I introduced us as the new owners of his old family property.

"I heard that someone from away had taken it on," he responded. "So it's you! I haven't been near it for years, not since I bought strawberries there. I hear it needs a lot of work."

"Frank's working on the plumbing and the electrician starts the rewire tomorrow," I shared.

"What about the insulation?" he asked.

I gave him a blank look.

"Better check that. Unless it's been changed, there's dried seaweed in the walls, and it's probably all sunk down to the bottom of the spaces. There's nothing in the top five feet of any outside walls. And the attic was bare, as I remember. No insulation up there."

The good news kept rolling in.

I asked how old the house was, to which he replied, "That's a long story. Listen! I'm off at six. That's our house next door. I always have a beer after work. You and your wife join us, and I'll answer any questions that I can."

We had an evening's essential housework planned, so we arranged to visit the next day.

In their large family kitchen, with the evening meal on the stove, Isaac and I took the first taste from the end of the working day beer. Barb was fascinated by the country kitchen, and was quickly distracted by Isaac's wife's offer of a look around the whole house.

"I grew up there, you know," was Isaac's opening statement from across the table. "There were 10 of us and I was the seventh. When dad died, we let mom have the house. When she passed, we sold it."

"How did your mom and dad feed the 10 of you?" I asked.

"Well, we fished. Everybody down the Passage and onto the island fished. There's an old government wharf at the end of your driveway. We had a cow for milk, couple of goats, chickens for eggs, and we grew all sorts of vegetables. That's why it was so easy to grow strawberries later. Dad and my grandfather, and probably his father before that, kept a small farm there. Lots of seaweed and lobster shells for fertilizer and more seaweed to insulate the new house, when it was built."

"New house?" I asked.

"Yes. The original one burnt down one January. My dad would often tell that story. That's how I know how old the house is. My dad was only seven when it happened, and he was born in 1875. In a couple of years, the new house will be 100 years old. The two add-ons that were to replace the kitchen came a little later."

Another drink and then he added, "For years after that fire, my mother swore that the place was haunted."

Barb's attention switched, as she returned from the tour of the Crozier's house.

"What happened?" I asked, trying to keep the excitement from my query.

"Mom swore that sometimes, late at night, she heard Uncle Bill coming down the stairs and into the kitchen. He'd open the oven on the old wood stove, and look for his boots that were often put in there overnight, to dry. That's how they think the fire started.

"Someone forgot to damp the fire down that night and the boots caught alight. Bill, who was never able to leave home, was my granddad's much younger brother. Herman and Elizabeth, my grandparents, got all the kids out: four girls and two boys, but the youngest died soon after. He was Bill, named after his uncle. Old Bill was awakened, but he never made it out of the building."

"Did you ever see or hear the ghost of Uncle Bill before you left there?"

"No!" Isaac laughed. "With 10 of us, the place was too noisy for ghosts. Dad never knew about it either. Mom only saw and heard it when she lived there alone, late in her life. She swore it was Uncle Bill. She spoke to him, but he never answered, just looked for his boots and went out the door."

"We saw him!" blurted out Barb. "The first two nights, before our furniture arrived, we camped out in the living room. Both nights, at about three-thirty, he came down the stairs, into the kitchen, looked for his boots in the oven, then left through a door that we still haven't been able to open."

"Did he say anything?" interjected Isaac's wife.

"It was strange," I answered. "He kept repeating the same two words, as if they meant a lot to him. He'd say, "My booooots!!" I tried to imitate the ghost's plaintive voice.

"Those are the only two words your mom ever heard him say," said Lois.

Her husband nodded in agreement. He told us that his mother only saw Bill at those times when the once bustling house was quiet, usually very late at night

He continued. "Dad always said the fire happened in the small hours of that January morning, probably about half past three."

It was quiet for a moment. Isaac interrupted, laughing, as he said, "Wait till I tell my brothers and sisters about this! Like me, none of them were ever quite sure about mom's ghost."

He went on to tell us that his family first settled our property in Shore Section, sometime after his widowed great-great-grandmother came from Barrington in 1830. She, her own children and some of the 13 her husband's first wife had borne, were on the 1838 census record as living there. The original house had probably been built about then

His wife asked one more time if we wanted to stay for supper. Regretfully, we had to decline. All the work we had to do and a meeting with the electrician took priority. Besides, we'd had the mystery of our "visitor" solved and we knew more than the bare bones of our new house's history.

Over the three years that we lived there, Isaac, and others, whose families had lived in the community for generations, put flesh on the property's historical bones. Some even believed the story of the ghost, which I only told after the rum bottle came out, by which time I no longer cared if my "I don't believe in ghosts" position was threatened by the telling.

Did Uncle Bill ever reappear?

One night, when Barb was away in Montreal, I thought I heard something downstairs. But we had two cats and I assumed one of them was down there eating. The oven door of the old, old stove we'd retained and restored was open the next morning. When Barb got back she asked why the door at that end of the kitchen was unlocked. It was still a door we never used and the key to the replacement lock we'd fitted was still hung on the nail, hidden in the kitchen cupboard.

When my teenage children visited, my daughter slept downstairs. One morning, she asked who'd come down to the kitchen in stocking feet and then gone out of the door in the middle of the night.

That evening, we lit a fire down on the beach, and I told them the story of Uncle Bill's Boots. They assumed it was one of the ghost stories that I often made up.

I think it's the only one that I might just believe in myself.

Postscript:

The house exists. The original was destroyed by fire. It was the home of the land grantees, the Kenney family. I don't know if there was ever a Bill in the family. One of the Kenney's did run the local service station. He told me about the fire as he pumped gas for us one day.

It took us two years to restore the house and tame the undergrowth that threatened to engulf it. We loved the summers, but the winters were hard. We became as much a part of the community as anyone did who "came from away", unless the "away" was Cape Breton. But we missed city proximity and conveniences and we did not have the many skills needed to improve the century old house. "The Crude but Effective School of House Restoration" had reached its limits.

We painted it blue, kept the surrounding grass trimmed and the alders at bay. We canoed and even tried swimming off our property. I think that was our final mistake. Lakes are to swim in. Everybody on the shore knows that. Besides, I didn't hunt, was bored by fishing lakes and streams, and you wouldn't get my seasick prone body on the ocean in a Cape Island boat.

We put the house on the market, and it sold to Montrealers looking for a summer retreat. We met them but, for fear of jeopardizing the sale, I did not tell this fictional story.

The now 130-year-old house is still used by the Montrealers every summer. In the winter, it's cared for by a neighbour. It shares the land with an all-weather tennis court and a boathouse, where winters a Cape Islander cruiser. There is also a newly built, luxury house on the shore, next to the "new" old Kenney House. The owner keeps the older house for the younger overflow of summer visitors she invites.

One story says that she built the newest one because field mice kept infesting the old house.

I wonder if their rustling at night might disguise the sounds of poor old Bill, still looking for "My Boooooots!" in the decorated and enamelled, wood burning range that still dominates one end of the kitchen.

~~~***~~~

Making it Happen

Art White

Our beautiful boy came quietly into the world on July 1, 1978, my twenty-fourth birthday. His eyes were mine; the red mop up top came from his Scottish father. We called him Joules (pronounced jewels), a term electricians, like his dad, toss about when talking shop. When Hansen McPherson first held his ruby-haired son and gazed down on his own likeness looking back, my rough-cut husband whispered ever so gently, "Oh, Ruby, he's a jewel, a God-given jewel...."

Joules was the apple of all our eyes, including his older sister, Ruby, who shares my name, or did until her baby brother dubbed her "Rudie" and it stuck. In turn, she, three days short of being his senior by four years, called my newborn her "Darling Child" and it fit.

DEUTERONOMY *SAYS,* "He found him in a desert land, in the howling wilderness and led him about, instructing him, keeping him as the apple of his eye." The prophet, *ZECHARIAH, ENLARGED THE ENDEARMENT,* "Thus saith the Lord of hosts... he that touches you touches the apple of his eye." Joules was God-given all right, and his gift rubbed off; he touched us, drew us out, and brought us deep, leaving an inner satisfaction, pleasure and peace.

During breakfast on our shared birthday in 1997, Joulie told me, "This may be our last birthday together for a while, Mum. I'm going west with Reg to join Larry. He got us jobs paying twice what we're making here. I just gotta give'er a try, at least earn a wad of money so's I can come back and live in the basement 'til the pogey runs out." He was his usual light-hearted, fun-making self, but I tell you, Joules' announcement settled like a cannonball in the womb that bore him.

I reached for his hands, squeezing back tears as my brand new 19-year-old said words that thereafter became a soothing mantra in good times and bad: "We'll always be together on Our Day, Mum, I'll make it happen." Typical Joules. "I'll make it happen." He'd said it ever since preschool and always seemed to deliver. Joules had me believing he'd do it now.

And he did. The next year I received a single, long-stemmed rose at my door with the card, "*Lo, a Rose E're Blooming.*" We never figured how he got the florist to deliver on a holiday. Three days later, his big sister opened her door to a singing messenger bearing 20 pink carnations: "*One for each year of being your Darling Child.*"

He was intimately thoughtful.

The next year it was a registered letter: "*Do not open until our birthday!*" It contained a $400 gift certificate to the Pines Resort Hotel. On the backside he'd scribbled, "*Take Dad out for a day of golf and fine dining, then stay the night.*"

Rudie got her own hand-delivered letter, also with a cheque for $400. "*You said your arms were too short to read the phone book. Here's half a day's pay to buy some fancy glasses for old folks. Your Darling Child.*" It was like he was right there with us.

On Halloween Day, 1999, at five in the morning, the phone startled us awake. It was Larry Feener. Joulie had died in a bunkhouse fire at the tar sands site, along with their best friend and schoolmate, Reg Conners. I can hear young Larry's quivery voice in my head right this minute.

Joules, our darling child, the apple of our eyes, was gone in a phone call, snuffed out like a cigarette under a shoe-heel. I never recovered. We never recovered. No one does. We know that now. But, in the strangest of ways, none of us feel without him either. It's as if Joules is just out at the cottage for the weekend.

The next year, on the July day Joules had said we'd always be together, I got up early. I planned to start some bread, then pick a bumper crop of sugar snaps in the cool of the forenoon.

"Hey, what's going on here?" There were no lights in the kitchen, no red numerals on the stove, no hum of the fridge. The rest of the house had power—the kitchen was dark. I put off making bread, telling myself, *Hansen'll fix it*, and went out to pick the peas.

"I can't find anything wrong," he said when I returned, consternation written across his tired face. "Let's go to the cottage

146

for your birthday, Ruby. This'll all be here when we get back." We wrapped the fridge and freezer in blankets to save the frozen food and headed to the Lake. The next morning, we returned to a kitchen bright with lights and a glowing burner on the stove. Unaccountably, all the clocks had kept perfect time.

A year-to-the-day later, we woke to the same scene: power everywhere but the kitchen. With hesitation, Hansen said, "When this happened on your birthday last year, I got to thinking. Joules re-did the wiring in that kitchen for your birthday, remember? Said an electrician's house ought not blow a fuse when the microwave and toaster are going at the same time. 'Sorta like a cobbler's kids going shoeless,' he said. Remember?"

I did, and I remembered, *We'll always be together on our Day, Mum. I'll make it happen....* Could it be? Just a coincidence? Hansen couldn't find anything amiss either time. The blackouts occurred, and lasted, only one day a year. The clocks never lost time that day either.

I phoned Rudie and told her what her dad and I had been talking about. "Oh, sure," she said, "I thought that the first time you told me, Mom. Somehow he's always with us; it's no coincidence. I feel him now. I can't wait 'til next year when we can test the theory, can you?"

I didn't know what to say, and when I did I wasn't sure. "I can't speak for your father, Rudie, but... I'm not planning to be home on my next birthday. There's no theory to test. I'm satisfied knowing what I know...."

Postscript:

"Making it Happen" is based on a real family with a "real" paranormal experience, including the son's death as described and his yearly "visitations." I was told this story in the nineties. I have taken literary license to make a story shell for this amazing sequence of facts, commonly held to be true. Names are contrived.

~~~***~~~

In Good Company

Janet Doleman

<u>Scene 1 – Date Night</u>

As the crow flies, the Mount Pisgah Cemetery is less than a quarter-mile from Andy Murray's farm. To get there by car, one has to take the main road for about a half-mile and turn onto the tree-lined lane leading into the cemetery, which is set back in a clearing in the woods. Mount Pisgah is a pleasant enough place in the daylight, with stands of birch and maple accenting groups of headstones, and grassy lanes running in between. A sharp turn at the front of the cemetery requires the large, hulking hearses to do a three-point turn to navigate the corner.

Behind the farm, a dirt road leads to a small, abandoned quarry, deep and filled with water. It lies in a hollow where the road ends at a large shelf of granite known as the Big Rock. It's a popular spot for impromptu picnics or just lazing on the sun-warmed surface. The rock and quarry are surrounded by a mixed brush forest of spruce, fir, and hardwoods, with one huge old oak tree standing above the rest, having withstood the winds of coastal storms and generations of climbing children. Neighbourhood kids hang out there. It's their swimming hole in summer, skating rink in winter, and the site of innumerable games of hide-and-go-seek, or King-of-the-Castle. The rules laid down by parents state they are never to go there alone, and to always be on the watch for snakes, which might be enjoying their own sun baths in the crevices of the Big Rock.

***

This cemetery is pretty enough in the daytime, Jimmy thought, as he geared down and turned into the tree-lined lane. He'd been to Mount Pisgah before to visit his grandfather's grave, so he was familiar with the neat groupings of gravestones separated by narrow grassy laneways and shaded by the occasional tall spruce, sturdy maple, and white birch.

Jimmy also knew it was a favourite place for guys to bring their girlfriends on Friday nights, slipping the chain off the gate ahead of time, and dimming the headlights as they drove toward the secluded glade. Tonight, with Marie finally agreeing to go out with him, here they were, doing exactly the same thing.

Marie sat on the far right of the front seat, hands demurely folded in her lap. She was the second-prettiest girl in his class; the first was already going steady with Kenneth Colson. As he drove up the lane, he glanced her way and was rewarded with a shy smile. When they reached the cemetery grounds, he carefully navigated the sharp turn and proceeded along a lane, stopping near a grove of birches. It was perfect timing: the sun had gone down and the last light in the western sky had faded to nothing. The only light was from the car headlights.

"This is a real nice place at night, with a great view of the stars," began Jimmy.

"Oh, do you come here often?" asked Marie, innocently, it seemed to Jimmy.

"Ah, well, no...some of the guys have been here...," he haltingly said, "and I've really only been here with my folks to see my grandfather's grave. It's over there, past those trees."

"Mmmm," she strained to see. "I can't really see much past the car lights. Maybe we can come in the daytime," she suggested. "Maybe you could show me where he's buried sometime...if that's all right with you."

"Sure, sure...anytime." Jimmy was eager to grasp another opportunity to spend time with the lovely Marie. "I'd just have to see about getting my dad's car." He paused. "But at night, when you turn off the lights, you can see the stars, millions of them. Want to try it?"

"Um...well, okay, but just for a few minutes. I have to be home by ten o'clock. My folks are pretty strict about that."

Jimmy turned off the engine, left the lights on for a minute longer, then dramatically turned off the switch.

"Ooh! I'm scared!" Marie said with a giggle. She inched a little closer to Jimmy. He wondered if she'd been here before.

Blackness closed around the car like a cloak. The streetlights along the main road were too far away to cast even a faint glow. It was very dark. The car's engine noises died away, and the only sound was their breathing and the squeak of Jimmy's leather jacket as he raised his right arm and laid it along the back of the seat.

"Um...can you see the stars?" asked Jimmy.

"Not really," said Marie. "It's so dark, and there's kind of a fog or mist or something. I don't remember seeing a fogbank this afternoon. It usually comes inland around suppertime."

Hmmm. Jimmy noticed wisps of mist in front of the car, just barely discernible in the dark. It seemed to get thicker. There were no stars visible, nor anything else. Where had this fog come from?

"Maybe we'd better go," suggested Marie, with a slight tremor in her voice. "I don't think there are any stars out tonight."

Jimmy sensed her nervousness and reluctantly withdrew his arm. "I guess you're right. It's getting late and I wouldn't want you to be grounded." He didn't say that he hoped they'd go out again soon.

"Why don't we come back another night, and bring chairs or a blanket, and a thermos of hot chocolate, when we know it's going to be a clear night?" said Marie. Jimmy could hardly believe what he was hearing.

"Good idea, I'd really like that." He tried to keep his voice neutral. He reached for the key to start the engine, then turned on the lights.

Suddenly, Marie screamed. Jimmy's mouth dropped open, but he couldn't make a sound. Marie scooted up against him and clutched his arm tightly.

The headlight beams shone directly at, or through, two figures in front of them. Jimmy's first and only thought was to get out of there, fast. The next thing he knew, he'd gunned the engine, and shifted wildly as the tires spun, lurching the car around the awkward turn at the front of the cemetery. Little pings rang out as gravel hit the two tombstones near where they'd been parked.

As the red taillights receded, the two figures remained, wavering and fading in the mist. One was wearing a type of uniform, the other in regular work clothes. They gazed at the grassy area below their feet, where two tombstones stood side by side. The mist thickened and swirled about until they were no longer visible.

Scene Two – The Call

The usual Saturday night supper was baked beans and brown bread at Jimmy's house. Charlie and Eva Spencer and their four children clustered elbow to elbow around the kitchen table, busily eating and passing dishes back and forth. The telephone jangled harshly, one long ring followed by two short.

"That's OUR ring!" piped up five-year-old Judy. She was not yet allowed to answer the phone, nor could she reach the brown wooden telephone box mounted in the front hallway.

Charlie got up to answer the phone. Eva could barely hear his muffled comments. "I'll be there as quickly as I can." He replaced the receiver, pausing briefly before returning to the kitchen. His eyes told Eva that something serious was happening, but he merely said, "That was Andy. He needs me down at the farm. Could be a while."

He reached for the old plaid jacket he wore in the woods and at grass-burning time. He shoved his feet into rubber boots and grabbed his work gloves. "Jimmy, I need you to stay here and help your mother with the younger ones."

Charlie glanced at his wife. "Maybe keep the kids inside after supper, Eva?" The tone of his voice telegraphed a note of concern to her. "I'll be back as soon as I can."

The door banged shut behind him. They heard the gravel crunch. Jimmy resumed eating, restlessly glancing at the clock. He would have to call Marie and cancel their date.

Scene Three – At the Farm

The engine groaned as Perley geared down to urge the old truck up the steep grade. The tires slipped on loose stones and gravel, and the wood-slatted sides rattled as the vehicle jolted over the larger rocks. Ahead, at the end of the long dirt drive, squatted a small white frame house, partially hidden by huge sheltering chestnut trees.

"This here section washes out every rainstorm," Perley announced knowledgably to his two passengers. There was no reply, nor any further comments.

The truck's bench seat barely contained the three occupants. On the right, his forearm resting on the open window, sat Joe Peary, a large man wearing dark suit pants and a rumpled white shirt. His necktie was loosened. Joe Peary was the local magistrate and part-time sheriff. His commanding presence struck fear and respect into the trembling, hat-in-hand penitents who appeared before his bench.

In the middle perched the slight form of Dr. Johnson, commonly known as the Doc. He clutched the handles of his black bag so tightly his knuckles appeared white, as if he was afraid it would be snatched from his grasp. Long experienced with local house calls to tend expectant mothers, feverish children or bedridden elderly folk, Doc suspected that all of his professional training might be called to bear before the night was through.

At the wheel, Perley Smith concentrated on steering and shifting, his eyebrows pulled down in a frown. Although stocky in build, agile Perley was adept at any odd job that might be asked of him. He could deliver your groceries, pick up a large parcel at the Post Office, mow, rake or trim lawns, and could take in-laws to the bus depot at a moment's notice, all for a modest fee. Despite the rattling from the back end, Perley's truck was his pride and joy. He kept it in good running order, because he never knew when he'd be asked to do a job that only he and his truck could handle.

"Drive 'round back," ordered Joe curtly, after they crested the hill and followed the dirt lane past the house. Late afternoon shadows stretched long across the yard, as the sun dropped behind a stand of dark spruce and pine. Whispering leaves stilled as the breeze died. Wooden pins lined the empty clothesline, the sheets, towels, socks, and pants long-since gathered into baskets before the evening damp threatened to coat them.

The truck pulled up next to the long, low building housing the chick hatchery. Andy Murray, farmer and deacon at Zion Baptist Church, waited. He nodded at the three men.

"Well, Andy?" asked Joe as he opened his door and got out.

"Just waitin' for Charlie to get here. We might need his help," said Andy in his measured drawl. "Called him a few minutes ago."

The four men stood silently near the rough-shingled wall of the outbuilding, while they looked at the disused wooden hay cart and at the red tractor, but not at each other. Perley scuffed one toe in the dirt and jingled coins in his pocket, but abruptly stopped when a glance from Joe cast a judgment that even that frivolous noise was unnecessary, perhaps flamboyant, while waiting for their task to begin. They knew Joe would fill them in on the details of why they'd been summoned, but only when Joe was good and ready.

They looked up as car headlights bobbed up the lane, punctuated by sounds of a struggling engine and tell-tale clatter of loose stones.

"Finally," Perley mumbled. Twilight was fast approaching.

Andy stepped forward as Charlie pulled up and shut off the engine. When he got out, he glanced from one to another, seeking an explanation to his sudden summons.

"Well," said Joe, "we'd better fill in Charlie on why we asked him for his help. It's getting dark and we need to get going. Andy?" Joe directed his gaze at the tall, stoop-shouldered farmer.

Andy cleared his throat and looked at the ground, avoiding the other men's eyes.

"I found somethin' in the woods." He paused. The men waited for Andy to continue. They knew better than to rush him through a story.

"Me and Ike here," he indicated with a nod at the black Lab at his feet, which looked up at him with a brief tail thump at the sound of his name. "Me and Ike were out looking for Roxy, my heifer. She gets out of the pasture every so often, and she went missing this afternoon. We set off for the thicket near the brook, where Roxy likes to hide herself. She sometimes gets into trouble in the swampy spots. I took this rope along to pull her out in case she was stuck."

"We were almost to the brook where it comes down from the old quarry, when he started growling and snapping his teeth. Now, Ike never does that with Roxy. He knows his job, to sniff her out and wait for me to lead her back." Andy tapped the coiled rope against his leg. The men waited.

"All I had with me was this here rope. I never thought of takin' the .22. It's been years since that cougar sighting. Ike knows to steer clear of skunks and porcupines, so this was strange. I didn't know what was up with him." Andy cleared his throat again, unused to such a long speech.

"Ike kept up his growlin' and pointed his nose at the dense brush around that huge old oak tree. He and I started over, slow-like, Ike growling the whole time, takin' care not to make too much noise in the brush. Just when we got close, Ike started to barking, short sharp barks. I haven't heard him bark like that since, well, since the whole herd got out through the broken fence, about five years ago."

"Well, *then* what? What was it?" Perley couldn't help himself.

"Shush," said Joe. Perley shushed.

Andy said slowly, "Well, it wasn't a cougar. I saw something blue, and something else, whitish." He paused for a second. "No animal I know is that colour. So, I took firm hold of Ike's collar and we pushed through the undergrowth until we got to the old oak. That's when I saw it."

"It?" squeaked Perley.

"Shush, Perley! Let Andy finish!" Charlie spoke for the first time.

"I hope to never see that sight again." Andy shook his head from side to side, and brought his hand up to his hat as he told them about his discovery.

***

Doc tightened his grip on the black bag. Charlie let out a low gasp and Perley a louder, "Ohhh," as if he'd been punched in the gut. Joe Peary stood motionless before speaking slowly and firmly in his deliberate, calm manner.

"Okay. Now you know what we're here for. Andy did the right thing—he went straight back to the house and called me. Then I got hold of Doc and Perley. Perley, do you have those tarps in your truck?"

Perley nodded. "Yes, sir. Always keep extra ones, just in case…." His voice trailed off, momentarily and uncommonly at a loss for words.

"Doc, you know what needs to be done. You and I are doing the police work on this. I got hold of the station sergeant up in Yarmouth; their men are tied up with a case and can't get here. Andy, you and Charlie and I will be the muscles. We'll need a knife, more rope and a lantern." Andy disappeared into the barn.

"Now, we'd better get going, or it'll be dark before we get there. Doc, you and Charlie ride up in the cab with Perley. Andy and I'll climb in the back. We'll take the truck up the quarry road as far as she'll go, then walk the rest of the way."

Andy reappeared with the requested items plus a pair of black rubber boots. "These here should fit the Doc," he said. "He'll need them where we're going." Andy called to Ike, bent and lifted him into the truck bed. They all climbed in.

"I told Mae to keep the children inside," said Andy.

"Good idea," said Joe.

Not one of the men uttered the thoughts foremost in their minds, as the truck crept along the narrow, rutted cart track. They realized their task would be grim, and Joe's even more so.

The diminishing evening light made the underbrush blacker and impenetrable to the naked eye. Branches scraped eerily along the truck sides, causing Perley to wince slightly as he navigated the ruts in the gathering dusk. Each man thought about their families and about the children who played innocently in these woods, silently grateful that it was Andy and his dog who had chanced upon their grisly discovery.

Perley braked, ground the gears and silenced the engine.

"This is as far as she'll go," he declared. "Out we get."

The men clambered out, gathering up the tarps, tools and rope. Andy grabbed the lantern, patting his breast pocket for matches. Doc stooped to pull on the boots, which came up to his knees.

"Andy, you lead with Ike. We'll fall in behind. Remember, no one touch anything when we get there, until Doc Johnson has a look."

The men nodded grimly, resigned to their mission, not questioning Joe's leadership.

"Let's get this done."

After their journey into the woods, the lantern-led procession arrived back at the farmhouse to be met by a policeman who'd finally arrived after confusing directions sent him onto wrong turns on country lanes in the dark. His black and white cruiser seemed out of place beside the barn. Mercifully, it had been camouflaged by nightfall as it navigated the steep lane. Joe Peary was relieved to see the uniformed officer, which meant that his responsibility was lightened and shared. After they transferred their burden from Perley's truck to the accompanying hearse, protocol was followed, details re-told and forms were completed.

Scene Four – Reunion

The forlorn little group gathered beside the open grave, weak sunlight shining on their bowed heads. Falling leaves drifted to lie gently on the still-green grass, dropped to the mound of fresh earth, and alighted on polished granite headstones. On the perimeter of the scene, the undertaker waited respectfully beside his vehicle. Farther away stood the caretaker, hat in one hand, shovel in the other.

Jimmy stood beside his father, Joe Peary and Andy Murray, apart from the grieving parents. He watched the husband in his grey Sunday suit, hat clutched to his chest, his arm around his wife's shoulders. The faint words of the minister reached his ears, "...dust to dust...," a sanitized version of death's immediate aftermath. What his father and the other men had discovered had been transitioned to a stark rectangle cut sharply into the earth.

For once, Charlie had overruled his wife's protests, allowing Jimmy to accompany him to the graveside service. They were the only attendants at this sad farewell. Their wives stayed at home and prepared small offerings of comfort—covered casseroles and collections of sweets on china plates—to take to the couple later on.

Jimmy thought about his dad and the other men, and what they'd found. He wondered exactly what had happened, since his father did not tell him the details. *Nor would he*, thought Jimmy. His imagination tried to fill in the gaps in what he knew. For the first time in his life, he allowed himself to wonder what it was like for grown men to be fathers and to know other men who had lost their sons.

Jimmy noticed a small tree nearby; it was an oak sapling, rare for this part of the county. He and his buddies had climbed the big oak tree near the quarry countless times. The woods near the old quarry were not far from where they stood in the cemetery glade. *As the crow flies...,* thought Jimmy.

As the group dispersed, Jimmy wandered away from the older men. He avoided looking at the deep hole or at the heavy casket, and tried not to notice the caretaker preparing to shovel the displaced earth into the open grave. He looked for the exact spot he'd been a few nights previously. He hadn't told his father about what had happened in the car that night, because he wasn't sure how to explain what they had seen.

He edged closer to the headstones on the far side of the new grave and tried to read the inscriptions on the two identical stones. He glanced at his father, who was engrossed in a conversation with the other men. He stooped and noticed that one stone was engraved with a military cross, plus a name and dates. The other stone bore the same last name, and only the years of birth and death. *What a short life*, he thought. *He wasn't much older than I am.* There was no stone yet for the newest grave. He'd overheard his dad's comments to his mom after he returned from the farm that night. They spoke in hushed tones of shock and sadness, the words, "...a horrible tragedy..." barely audible.

Gravestones tell only part of the story. Jimmy figured that the older people in the community knew all about family histories, or thought they did. Secrets can outwit the cloak of night in small communities, seep over telephone lines, and root in neighbours' houses, accumulating truths and half-truths along the way.

He thought about the two ghostly figures he and Marie had seen. *Perhaps at night, when the cemetery was once again peopled by ethereal beings, they get together to take inventory and meet up at the most recent graves to share tidbits of ghostly gossip.* He could almost hear them saying, *"Did ya hear about this one? They said he was a handsome young devil, but up to no good. Too bad, so sad, he shoulda known better. He coulda been someone! Ha! Well, at least they're all together now, toes up and all that. See y'all next moonrise!"* The imagining helped divert his thoughts away from the open grave and its new occupant.

Jimmy didn't know how eerily accurate this was. Late that night, long after the cars had left and the cemetery was quiet, a dense milky mist crept through the thickets, entwining threadlike wisps around the little sapling, creating floating wreaths around the pinnacles of ornate tombs. Gradually, two wavering figures took shape, one in a type of uniform, the other in ordinary work clothes. Instead of gazing at the ground below, they appeared to be chatting together. The mist swirled at their feet, rising into a third shape, shorter than the other two, clad in a loose shirt and dungarees, a cap perched on the back of his head. These three hovered for a while above the two older graves and the mound of earth topped by fresh flowers, and chuckled together, as if sharing a joke or funny story.

Not that there was anyone there to see.

~~~***~~~

158

Never Go Across to that Island

Tom Robson

I can't remember a summer I didn't visit my grandfather's cottage. I still go there, even though it's been years since he died. The cottage has lots of memories, but the one I will never forget happened on a hot, August day, when I was 14.

Mom, Dad, and Grandpa had gone into town. My sister, who was 15 and never missed a chance to go shopping, went with them. I was supposed to go, but I persuaded Grandpa and Mom that it was safe to leave me alone; I would be careful and wouldn't do anything wrong, foolish, or dangerous. I would have promised them anything to get out of a boring 15-kilometre trip to the three-aisle supermarket and on to the hardware store.

But I soon discovered it was just as boring back at the cottage when I couldn't go near the lake, or ride Grandpa's ATV, or go through the woods to the top of the bluff. Of course, there was no television out there, and computers and phones were a long way from being today's electronic devices. Grandpa's old dog wouldn't even wake up to play with me.

I walked down to the dock and gazed across the lake. I dared not go out in the boat with the outboard, but what harm was there in going for a paddle in grandpa's canoe? I would wear a lifejacket and I was used to paddling it alone. No one would know. The sun was shining; there was no wind and there were very few clouds in the sky. It was great paddling weather.

I grabbed a lifejacket and the paddle Grandpa had made for me. I put a bottle of water and some cookies in my backpack. I had at least two hours before the family came back and, besides, I wasn't going far.

I locked the cottage, hid the key in its usual place, and began a trip I wish I had never taken.

Once in the canoe, I had my second foolish idea. Grandpa had always said, "Never, ever go to that island just off Beaver Point." I'd heard that said to every visitor, kids and adults, every year, at least four times a year. The explanation was that it "isn't safe! In fact it is really dangerous there!" Grandpa said it was haunted. His stories would have you believe that the ghost of Silas the Miser, who had lived on the island for years, and who had died there, kept people from finding his hoard of money. He also claimed that the island was booby trapped.

But there the island sat, only about 200 metres away, just off the Boutilier's property. Such an easy paddle to the beach in that little cove facing me: a place to land and pull up the canoe. What was in those trees covering the island? Perhaps somebody had lived there since Silas because there were the remains of a dock beside the beach, and a sort of path leading from it.

My idea was that this was the time to explore the small island. It was perhaps 200 metres long and less than that wide. Perhaps I'd find a clue to Silas' treasure. Why didn't Grandpa want me to visit this mysterious place? I was intrigued.

Two hours would give me lots of time to paddle out there, explore, and paddle back. What could be dangerous in that? Unless Grandpa or my parents found out, and that wasn't going to happen.

It was an easy paddle to the island. I beached the canoe and then I made my next mistake. I didn't tie it up. I was so keen to walk up that overgrown path that I didn't bother. I scrambled through the tangle of underbrush and spruce trees until I spotted something ahead that looked like the ruins of a building. Any thoughts of ghostly traps and pitfalls had gone from my mind.

The building had once been a house, but the roof, at one end, had collapsed. There were no windows left and the door leaned open on one hinge. I wondered if it was safe to go inside and what I might find.

Then I heard something that didn't quite belong. There were noises coming from behind the house. There was a clanking noise, but in the background was the sound of bells. For a moment I remembered the story of the ghost. But I dismissed the thought. I didn't believe in ghosts anyway.

So I made yet another mistake. I didn't turn round and paddle back home. Instead, I struggled round the side of the ruin to peep behind. The noises were coming from high up in an ancient maple tree; I spotted some wind chimes and several heavy metal pieces hanging and clanking against one another in the freshening breeze. *Nothing to be scared of,* I thought.

It was then I noticed what looked like a stone poking above the grass and weeds in a small area that someone had tried to keep clear.

Once I'd cleared the grass and other debris away, I could see that it was a gravestone, and it had writing carved into its face—a lot of writing. It took me quite a while to scrape the lichen and moss off the stone so I could read what was written. I know what it said because, once I'd read it, I copied it down on a piece of paper crumpled in the bottom of my backpack. There were two types of carvings. The words etched crudely at the bottom, not as deep or clear as those at the top, were more difficult to read.

Here lies
SILAS CRAWFORD.
September 13th 1864 - October 31st 1953.
They say I save and never spend.
My money's safe, you can depend.
I never gave. I didn't lend.
I used it well. No one can find,
Though many tried, the money that I left behind.
And he that looks shall be left blind.
My treasure is for all mankind.

He lies! Silas the Miser kept it with him.
It's here, somewhere.
Take care! He guards it still.

Even if my name had not been Colin Crawford, the tombstone messages would have intrigued me. I'd gone this far; why not use the time I had left to look farther? Maybe there was a fortune hidden here.

My errors were mounting up. The sun had gone in and clouds were gathering as the wind crept even into the sheltered, scrub-crowded clearing. None of that caught my attention in my eagerness to get into that ruin of Silas the Miser's home, to start my search for treasure.

The back door, leading into the part of the house where the roof was almost intact, also hung open. As I looked through it, I saw that daylight crept in through empty window frames as well as holes in the roof and walls. I didn't think about what could be lurking in the shadows. There was enough light to go in and explore.

I should have been more cautious, but I wasn't.

I stepped in through the doorway, forgetting to check the floor. Two steps in and it gave way. I went crashing into what must have been the basement. I crashed onto a hard floor, all the breath knocked from my body and one leg crumpled beneath me. Thank goodness I still had the lifejacket on. I think it saved my back and ribs.

I lay there, the light barely able to penetrate the hole I'd made above me. I tried three or four times to sit up, but I couldn't. My leg wouldn't let me.

When I tried to straighten it to make movement easier, it really hurt. I felt around for something that would help me haul myself into a sitting position. There was nothing, only spongy wood and some other, harder pieces. I picked one up and held it to the dim light.

It was a bone, a long bone.

I screamed and threw it away. Somehow I straightened my leg, though it was agony to do so. Then I sat up, leaning back on my elbows. Half stunned, I peered into the indistinct corners. Was something or someone moving in the darkest of them? Had the ghost of Silas brought me to this perilous situation? Was his spirit protecting his fortune from treasure hunters like me? I shivered as I tried to dismiss these haunting thoughts from my mind. That's when I saw the first rat.

Before my imagination ran riot and created more fear, it was disturbed by a bright flash of light that showed the remains of stairs against the far wall.

Almost immediately there came the clap of thunder and then the rain. But it wasn't just a shower. It was a sudden downpour that began to drench me, even in that half-sheltered basement.

The water began to flow down the walls and in through the floor above me. A few minutes later, at the height of the thunderstorm, I realized that the water was puddling around me. The basement was flooding. I should move.

I dragged my hurting body over to the staircase. My leg was useless as well as painful. When I reached the stairs and tried to drag myself up them, I realized the steps had rotted. They would not take my weight. I was trapped. There was no way out.

But the next lightning flash revealed water flowing down a ramp from another doorway, high up in the far corner. The hatch at the top of the ramp had gone. If I could crawl there, I could scramble up that ramp, if the water streaming down didn't stop me. As painful and difficult as it was, I had to try.

I attempted to crawl but the pain in my knee was excruciating and I must have passed out.

I came to in a pool of water.

The downpour was still flowing into the basement. Water was now about half a metre deep in places. If I collapsed into it, I could drown. Above me, on the rotten steps, were rats escaping the flood. I realized that the life jacket could help me get across the basement to that ramp. If I lied down, let my legs float, and used my hands on the floor to pull myself through the water, movement would be easy. Who knows what my hands touched and grabbed on that basement floor, but I made it and dragged myself a little way up the ramp.

That was as far as I could get. The ramp, even after the thunderstorm stopped, was too much for me. I couldn't drag myself out. It was too steep and slippery. One leg was useless and I was wet, cold, hurt, and exhausted. I must have passed out again soon after it got dark. My last thought was that this had to be the work of the ghost of Silas. I was caught in his trap.

I came to as I was dragged up the ramp and strapped onto a board. It was a backboard, brought in by the paramedics; my grandpa and father had found me the next afternoon and called them.

My family had returned from town in the middle of the thunderstorm and wondered where I was. They figured I'd been off walking and was sheltering until the rain stopped.

Mom was worried that I had been struck by lightning. Then, as the rain eased off, Grandpa noticed that the canoe was gone from the dock.

Before darkness fell, he and Dad got in the other boat, and began to look for the canoe. It wasn't where I'd dragged it up. Instead, they found it adrift in the lake.

Everyone feared the worst. I'd gone out in the canoe, gone overboard in the storm, and drowned. Grandpa started a search of the lakeshore and the island beaches while Dad and Mom drove round and got everybody on the lake to check their shoreline. Darkness fell and they hadn't found what they were looking for—my body. They all thought I had drowned.

Before dawn, Grandpa woke up with a brainstorm. He realized he had forgotten to check lifejackets. He saw that one was missing and hoped that I had been wearing it. At first light they began to check the shoreline and search the islands again. All the neighbours on the lake were helping. The police and Search and Rescue had been informed. Of course, the last island to be checked was the one Grandpa had warned me about. He'd assumed that I had heeded his warning and wouldn't go near the place.

Wrong!

But they followed my trail from the beach, through the brush, and to the tumbledown house of Silas Crawford.

They realized that someone had cleaned off the gravestone and decided to thoroughly check out the ruin. They found me lying on the bottom of the ramp: dehydrated, unconscious, and with torn knee ligaments.

I was first taken to the local hospital, then sent for surgery back in the city. I was on crutches for some weeks after surgery, until healing and the physio began to take effect. I would have been in a lot more trouble, except they'd found me alive, when they all believed I was dead.

In the hospital, Grandpa told me about the island, the house, and about his uncle Silas who had made a lot of money in the States. He'd come back, bought the island, and built his house there. He had become a recluse in his old age and refused to let anyone on his island, except his nephew, my grandfather, whom he'd befriended. All the locals thought that Silas was filthy rich, and even the family believed he was wealthy.

Eventually he died, alone, on his island, where he'd lived for the last 30 of his 89 years.

It had taken two years to find his will, which had been left in some safety deposit box in a Boston bank. During that time, treasure hunters trashed the house and scoured the island, looking for his hidden fortune. It had never been there. One of them must have carved the words on the bottom part of his tombstone some time later.

The will had revealed two things. The first had confirmed his oft-spoken wish to be buried on the island, with the words I'd seen carved on his gravestone. The second had been his desire to leave, anonymously, his considerable fortune towards the building and upkeep of our local hospital. His "treasure was for all mankind".

And why had my grandfather kept us all away from the island? He owned it, thanks to Silas' will. But a condition had been that no one could live on, or even visit the island. Grandpa had encouraged the ghost stories, even though Silas, when alive, had been far from evil. He was crotchety, rather than scary and mysterious.

But I had visited his island. I should have asked Grandpa to explain the story and then, maybe, he would have taken me to explore—safely.

But Grandpa did have the last word. He willed me Crawford Island. Same condition applies. Nobody can visit the island, unless I approve.

And no! I never did find that bone, or any others, in that basement when, for safety reasons, we had the old house torn down. I still paddle over there every summer, just to keep the gravestone clean.

This coming summer I plan to tell my son and daughter about their ancestor, Silas. I'll take them to visit his island and see his gravestone. And then I'll tell them about his ghost.

~~~***~~~

Eternal Love

Wilma Stewart-White

The view was what had drawn her to this house. Perched in the odd little dormer at the top of the house, Clare could see the heaving sea for miles and miles. The real estate dealer had told her the dormer was known as a Lunenburg bump. A funny name for her favourite spot, but she could see why a sailor's wife would want one. The view was spectacular on clear days.

Today, though, the beach was almost invisible through billows of fog. Stretches of sand appeared and disappeared. The unearthly notes of the nearby foghorn made her shiver.

"On a night like this anything could happen," she whispered.

As she watched, she was amazed to see figures on the beach.

"Who would willingly go out on a night like this?" she whispered to herself.

Perhaps she was imagining things—but no. Once again she saw them. A couple walking slowly along arm in arm. The woman was slightly bent over and seemed to be wrapped in a long cardigan. Her companion was so thin, he was almost transparent. They seemed oblivious to the inclement weather and the damp wisps of fog wrapped around them. As she watched, they disappeared down the far end of the beach. The maniacal laughter of the loons in the pond shattered the silence. She shivered.

"It's just a goose walking over my grave," she muttered, thinking about that silly phrase from her mother's time.

She jumped as her phone rang. It took a few seconds before she could pull herself into the moment to answer it.

"Hello," she croaked.

"Clare? Is that you?" It was her neighbour farther down the beach.

"Yes, yes, I was just miles away."

"Just wanted to know if you were ok in this first foggy night alone."

"Oh, yes," she answered. "I've been watching the fog on the beach. Tell me, who would I have just seen walking along the beach just now in this awful weather?"

"What! What do you mean? Walking along the beach now? Tonight?"

"Yes, an older couple who looked too frail to be even out in this weather," she answered.

There was silence on the other end of the line, long enough for Clare to think the connection was broken. "Are you still there, Anne?"

A deep breath came from the phone. "How about you come by for tea tomorrow morning and we can talk about your mirage?"

"Mirage? What do you mean?"

"Trust me. The story will be better in the sunlight. See you tomorrow." There was a sudden click as Anne hung up.

"Now there is a mystery!" mused Clare. She pulled the bright yellow curtains across the window and took her wondering thoughts elsewhere. With luck, the fog would be gone in the morning and her questions would be answered.

Just before she headed to bed, she took one last look out at the beach before her. Tendrils of fog played hide and seek with the full moon that sailed across the sky, but no figures could she see.

"My imagination?" she wondered aloud. She first picked up a mystery novel but her cat mewed at her. "Yes, you're right, a good English novel is what I need. No more mysteries for tonight."

Clare and the cat made for her comfy bed.

The next morning, the fog persisted as she walked down the little lane to Anne's cape house. With a warm and welcoming bright red door and a plume of smoke puffing from the central chimney, it looked like a house in a fairy tale.

She was glad she had chosen this tiny community. Everyone was busy and friendly. She knocked on the door and immediately heard the welcome barking of Queenie, Anne's rescue greyhound, at the same time Anne opened the door.

"Come in, come in," she beckoned warmly. "As you can hear, Queenie is glad for some company. I am not speaking to her; she demolished half my museum tea biscuits this morning."

Clare walked into the open room. Anne had removed some interior walls so she could see the beach and the grey ocean swells, or even down to the small freshwater pond with its flotilla of ducks, from almost anywhere in the room.

"What a wonderful vista."

"That and its age is what attracted us to the house. This house has watched the sea for over 200 years and has seen many storms and struggles on that beach."

Anne handed Clare a mug of tea. Clare wrapped her hands around the heat and inhaled the fragrance.

"Tell me Anne, what did I see last night? Real or imaginary?"

Anne sat beside her. "Well, it depends on you." Anne took a deep breath. "It sounds like you saw Janet and Philip walking the beach as they have for 30 years."

"So which house is theirs?" asked Clare.

"The house they used to live in is the grey one surrounded by rhododendrons just as you round the big curve."

"Used to live in.... Do you mean they moved?"

"In a manner of speaking." Anne sighed and studied Clare's face. "They both died last winter about this time."

Clare sat stunned by Ann's information. Her heart pounded faster.

"Died… but how? What are you saying?"

"I think," Anne said, "you saw their ghosts."

"Don't be ridiculous. There are no such things as ghosts." She paused as she gazed upon the serious expression on Anne's face. "Are there?"

"Let me tell you their story and you can draw your own conclusions."

Clare sat back, skeptical, but secretly wanted to hear more.

"Long ago, Janet and Philip moved to our little community. Philip had retired from the Navy and wanted to live by the sea. Their house had been built some years before by a sea captain who wanted a safe harbour to come home to. Philip felt the same. Janet was a writer of scholarly books and needed a quiet place to work. They added a studio to the old house and lived there happily. Every night they dined together by candlelight, then walked the beach together arm in arm planning their days. On windy days, she'd wrapped herself in a long woolen cardigan that had originally been his. Their children, grown and long gone, would visit from time to time but really they lived for each other. He read to her each evening. Every moment of their lives was lived in tandem. They even finished each other's sentences. Fall before last, though, Philip got ill; it was stage five colon cancer that had spread. Philip refused to stay in hospital except for treatment; care givers came to the house. Janet got thinner and thinner and more ethereal and grey as she watched over him. They kept their little rituals, even though they could no longer walk the beach. She ate on a tray beside his bed by candlelight. She read aloud to him in the evening. It soon became obvious that time was running out for Philip. Palliative care nurses began the watch.

"Janet and Philip had a ritual. All the years Philip was at sea with the navy, he carefully entrusted his grandfather's watch to Janet. He would place it in her palm and say, 'Keep this safe for me until we can wind it up together and start our life anew.' She would then walk the beach and watch the ocean upon which Philip had sailed as if she were on the voyage with him.

"Late one night, as he grew weaker, he called her close and asked for the watch. They carried out the ritual. She put the watch in her pocket to keep it safe. Soon, Philip fell into his final coma. As he slipped away, Janet followed her own path. She picked up the well-worn cardigan and went to the back door. She could see the moon high in the night sky. The night was fiercely cold. She wrapped her cardigan around her and made her way through the snow to her favourite place on the calm beach.

"She sat down and took out the watch. Oblivious to the cold and snow, she waited. As Philip moved into his eternal sleep so did she—a voyage shared.

"The next morning, an early dog walker found her snow-covered body at the same time an ambulance came for Philip's body. It was their last journey together, just as they had planned.

"On stormy or foggy nights, folks say they have seen them walking together on their beach, always arm in arm."

Clare exhaled. "What a story!" she exclaimed. "Is it true?"

"Oh, yes," Anne said and nodded. "Now the next part is up to you. Did you really see them last night or were they figments of your imagination? Only you know that."

Clare finished her tea and set down her cup. "I think I need to give this some deeper thought."

She set out for home, taking the beach path, the same one Janet and Philip frequented for so many years. She sat down on an old log and considered the story. As a naval officer's wife, she had her share of times alone. Right now, David was at sea in the Gulf. He had gone four months ago and would be gone another two or three before his crew were relieved. She knew well the aching hours of loneliness and the lack of strong arms around her. She was a busy and positive person, at least to the people around her, but deep inside she occasionally yearned for a life that included David with her each day.

She began to understand Janet and her choice. Sometimes a temporary absence could be borne bravely, but a final farewell might break your heart.

~~~***~~~

Neptune's Wraith
Phil Yeats

Storm clouds darkened the sky as a nor'easter gathered strength, sweeping the fog lurking off the headland into the bay. I hurried down to the dock to secure my dory.

Fog enveloped the little cluster of houses along the shore in Lower Priest's Harbour, but a lone boat called *Neptune's Wraith* was anchored not far from our dock, and quite visible in a small pocket of clear air. It looked low in the water and seemed to be rocking more than usual, as if a number of people were moving about on-board. Probably just the effect of the increasing wind and waves from the impending storm, I thought, as I turned my attention to Jessie, my granddaughter, and four of her friends approaching from the road. I could hear them clearly, but they were barely visible in the mist.

"Don't come down here!" I yelled, abandoning my efforts to tie down the dory. "It's too slippery. Go up to the house and see if Grandma can find you some cookies." A foggy February afternoon on a slippery dock was no place for kids.

Fifteen minutes later, Jessie stood in the doorway to our sitting room surrounded by her four little friends. "Hey, Grandpa, can you tell me and my friends a story?"

"Sure, honey, what sort of story would you like?"

"A ghost story," one of them suggested.

"I don't think I know any ghost stories. Would you like one about fishermen?"

"But you aren't a fisherman, Grandpa."

She was right. I wasn't a fisherman, or even a real Nova Scotian from the Eastern Shore. I'm a city slicker from away who worked for 35 years in a government office in Halifax. Muriel and I moved to the small fishing village of Lower Priest's Harbour after our daughter, Stephanie, married the son of a real Eastern Shore fisherman.

"But my fishermen stories are my best."

"No, we want a ghost story," she insisted.

"Okay, I do know one ghost story," I admitted, furiously trying to turn *Neptune's Wraith* into inspiration for a ghost story.

The five village kids gathered around my recliner. Two settled on the floor and the others bounced up onto our leather sofa.

"This is a real story and it took place before any of you were born, shortly after your grandma and I moved to the bay."

"Before Mummy married Daddy?" Jessie asked.

"No, we didn't move here until after your mum and dad were married. Now, will you let me tell my story?"

"Yes, we want a story!" exclaimed a little imp who could never keep still. As usual, he was pestering the two girls. My story would have to compete with their shrieks.

"With lots of ghosts," a more subdued boy wearing glasses added.

I put the book I'd been reading, *Relativity: the Special and General Theory* by Albert Einstein, on a table and settled into my tale. "It was late fall when a big sailboat, a Beneteau 37, sailed into the bay, and the crew did a very professional job of dropping the sails and swinging up to the mooring in front of our house. There was quite a wind blowing, but they managed without any need for their motor."

"It's an engine, not a motor," Andrew, the little guy with glasses, interjected with the disdain only a ten-year-old growing up in a fishing village could show for a landlubber.

"Engine, whatever. I was right here, reading this book, but distracted by the late season arrival in the bay. I watched as the crew cleaned up the boat and put away the sails."

"That was a long time ago," Jessie said. "It must have been a different book." They weren't letting me get away with anything.

"You're right. It was 12 years ago, so it must have been a different book. But I was here reading a book and watching the people on the boat when Mr. Duggan, the man who owns the mooring, rang the doorbell. He told me that the boaters were friends who planned to leave the boat in Priest's Harbour until the next summer."

"Was it a ghost boat?" Andrew asked.

"I don't know, but it was all white and called *Neptune's Wraith*," I said, stealing the name from the boat anchored in the bay. "Do you know what that means?"

"Sea ghost… it really was a ghost boat," Andrew said with a melodramatic shake in his voice. He'd given me a new idea; I needed to add a ghost boat to my story.

"So," I continued, "a little later the four people from the boat paddled their dinghy to the dock and tied it down very thoroughly so it wouldn't blow away during any winter storms."

"Rowed their dinghy," said Master Know-It-All, Andrew. "You row a dinghy, but paddle a canoe or kayak."

"Then, Mr. Duggan and the four sailors drove away in his Hummer," I concluded, ignoring Andrew's interjection.

"I need to pee," Alice said. "Don't tell any more until I get back."

I continued after all five children visited the bathroom.

"Nothing happened until one night in February. It was like today, cold and foggy, and the ice spread across the mouth of the bay and all around the shore. There was open water in the middle of the bay and *Neptune's Wraith* and the few other empty moorings were okay. It was dark, so we couldn't see anything, but we could hear the engine from a small ship. You know how it is when it's foggy; you can hear things, but it's hard to say where they are, or how far away. So, we couldn't tell exactly where the ship was, but it seemed to be just outside the harbour."

"Dark and foggy is good," said Andrew. The little guy was destined to be a storyteller when he grew older.

"Sorry, Andrew, but nothing supernatural happened. The next morning, the fog lifted and the Coast Guard ship, *Gannet*, pushed through the ice into the bay. Police cars sped down the road from Highway 7 and they searched the whole bay and visited all the houses and buildings along the shore. The Coast Guard even checked out the boat on the mooring.

"Before they left, the Coast Guard people said they were after four bad guys who were smuggling people into the country, people who shouldn't have been here. They'd chased their boat into Priest's Harbour the previous night but it had just disappeared. They looked everywhere, but there was no sign of the boat or the people."

"Wow! What happened to them?" Andrew asked. He was the only one really listening to the story.

"No one knows. That evening, I went to the Legion in Musquodoboit Harbour to learn if anyone knew anything."

"My mum says going to the Legion and drinking beer is bad." Alice said. Maybe they were listening more than I thought, but it was hard to tell with all the shrieking and bouncing about they were doing.

"Is that right? Well maybe you shouldn't tell her I went to the Legion."

"Is it really bad?" a wide-eyed Jessie asked.

"No, it's okay for grown-ups to go to the Legion and have a glass of beer. It's only bad if you have too many. Just like you guys, having one glass of pop is okay, but your mums don't let you have extra ones, do they?"

"What about the ghosts?" the single-minded Andrew asked.

"When I got to the Legion, everyone was talking about the Coast Guard and the police. Mr. Jennings said he looked out in the morning and one of the empty moorings was pulled over to the west like it had an invisible boat on it. Everyone teased him about that, saying there couldn't be a ghost boat out there. But he denied actually seeing a ghost boat. He said it was obvious no boat was on the mooring, so something else had to be pushing it to the side. But no one could say what it was, so you see, Andrew, it could have been a ghost boat that came in during the night."

"Awesome! But were there people on the ghost boat?"

"Well, maybe. Someone at the Legion said a dinghy tied to their dock had been moved, and there were footprints in the snow that no one could explain."

"But ghosts wouldn't make footprints," Andrew stated. He seemed very confident about his facts.

"One more thing. The next night, we heard another boat engine start up and leave the harbour, but no one ever saw a boat. So, Andrew, what do you think it all means?"

"It was a magical boat that was invisible and made everyone in it invisible as well, but as soon as someone got off the boat they became visible again."

"I think you might be right," I replied. His answer was at least as good as the one I planned to use.

"But Grandpa, that isn't a proper ghost story," Jessie complained.

"Why not?"

"Because a ghost story should have a haunted house or a scary graveyard and people need to be frightened by the ghosts."

"Well, sorry, it was the best I could do. Now I think it's time for everyone to go home for dinner."

Muriel helped the kids into their coats and boots and I escorted Jessie home, dropping the others off along the way.

"I don't mind that it wasn't a proper ghost story," Jessie said at her door.

"No, why not?"

"Because you tell us grown-up stories. We like it that you tell us grown-up stories."

***

The following afternoon I waited for Jessie where the school bus dropped the kids off. Muriel wasn't feeling very chipper, so I'd volunteered to give her a break by entertaining Jessie at Stephanie's house.

Mrs. Macintyre was waiting for Alice, her granddaughter. "Did you hear what George Jennings said this morning?" George was the village busybody and self-proclaimed expert on almost everything.

"No, Muriel's a bit under the weather so I've been at home all day on chicken soup patrol."

"Well, he said he watched 12 people, five men, four women, and three children walk past his house and up the road to Highway 7 just after dawn this morning. You know what that means don't you?"

"No, I'm not sure I do."

"That's right. You're from away and wouldn't know about the launch from a tramp steamer that foundered on the shoals guarding our inlet in 1962. It carried 12 foreigners, illegal immigrants, and they all drowned."

"Let me guess: five men, four women, and three children. But Jenning's house is well back from the road and it was foggy this morning. How could he be so sure about the numbers?"

"I don't know, maybe he was imagining some of the details," Mrs. Macintyre suggested.

"And what about the people in 1962, couldn't anyone save them?"

"No, the Coast Guard ship, *Gannet,* was nearby, but they couldn't save anyone."

"The *Gannet,* I didn't realize she was that old."

"It was her maiden voyage, and yesterday was the fiftieth anniversary of the disaster. George thinks he saw the ghosts of those 12 poor souls, and he's so put out he's been drinking in the Legion since it opened."

"What happened to the steamer?" I asked as Mrs. Macintyre watched the village kids getting off the bus. "Was anyone held to account?"

"Yes, the *Gannet* chased them down and the four ringleaders were arrested."

***

When I returned to my place after Stephanie got home, I made two interesting observations. Someone had launched my dory and tied it to the dock, and the real *Neptune's Wraith,* not the one in my story, once again rode high in the water. I figured I knew the origin of George's ghosts. These weren't weightless ghosts from 1962 that wouldn't leave any footprints; they were real people involved in a new human smuggling operation. They'd been smuggled into the bay the night before I told my story to the kids, and housed on *Neptune's Wraith.* Then, this morning before dawn, they were moved from the boat to the shore and away. George had seen them as they left the village.

But was my rational explanation correct, or could George be closer to the truth than anyone realized? I considered the eerie parallels between the 1962 disaster that I'd known nothing about, the story I told the kids, and the real situation unfolding within hours of me telling my story. Could these have been coincidences, or was a spirit sending me a message? Maybe there really were ghosts out there, just not the ones George thought he saw.

I had no choice. I had to tell my story, even though I would risk becoming the subject of ridicule. I had to provide the RCMP with my observations, and help them investigate this latest human smuggling episode.

~~***~~

Authors' Biographies

Russell Barton –

Russell taught creative writing at Algonquin College in Ottawa and at the Nova Scotia community college for 15 years. He published two textbooks on Writing Fiction; The Way of The Story, Part One and Part Two in 2000 for use in his classes.

Russ was managing editor for *A Drop in the Ocean* and *Jilted Angels*; both anthologies by Nova Scotian authors. He received a third place award at the 29th Annual Atlantic Short Story Writing Competition in 2006.

His story, "About Face" was published in The Vagrant Revue of New Fiction in 2007. Another short "Father Mooney's Christmas Surprise" was published by Nimbus in 2008.

Russell is happily married to artist Susan Feindel and they live in Dartmouth, Nova Scotia.

Manon Boudreau –

Manon grew up in the small town of Petit-Rocher, New-Brunswick. As the wife of an RCMP officer, Manon calls home whatever community welcomes her and her family. She started writing when her family was moved to Falmouth, Nova Scotia. She and her husband are blessed with three beautiful children, who make their daily lives a wonder. When she's not writing, she's most likely to be found entertaining her children, reading or enjoying a glass of red wine.

Being fluent in French and English, Manon takes pleasure in writing in both languages. Her education background is in Psychology and she has worked in the school system for some years.

Janet Doleman –

Janet grew up in the small community of Barrington Passage on Nova Scotia's South Shore. She remembers her grandmother's original poems in birthday cards, which inspired her to write. She carries on a family tradition of writing diaries, letters and journals. Janet earned her B.A. in English and a University diploma in Secretarial Science at Acadia University, Wolfville, NS, and lives in Dartmouth with husband George. Their daughter Katie lives and works nearby; son Michael works in law enforcement in British Columbia.

Maida Barton Follini –

Maida is a Connecticut Yankee transplanted to Nova Scotia in 1980. Her interests include Genealogy and History, and she edits a Family Newsletter circulated to over 100 kinfolk. While living in Amherst, Nova Scotia, Maida wrote a series on the history of churches in Cumberland County, and a monthly column for the Amherst Daily News. Her poem, "Osprey's Call" won the Cumberland County Library's poetry writing contest, and she has had several poems published in journals of the Religious Society of Friends (Quakers). Moving to Dartmouth, N.S. in 2008, Maida volunteers at the Dartmouth Heritage Museum, where she edits the Museum *Gazette*. She has authored the museum pamphlet "A Quaker Odyssey: The Migration of Quaker Whalers from Nantucket, Massachusetts to Dartmouth Nova Scotia and Milford Haven, Wales."

Diane Losier –

"A writer is someone for whom writing is more difficult than it is for other people." Diane Losier is in the process of discovering the truth in Thomas Mann's paradoxical statement. She still has her first journal entries neatly written, in pencil, at 10 years old. Her bedroom closet is full of the numerous journals she has filled over the years. Recently retired, Ms. Losier has taken several writing courses, including a semester in Writing Short Fiction at a local university in Halifax. Writing short stories has proven to be a challenge which she is, nevertheless, greatly enjoying. Her very first short story, "Changes", is included in this anthology.

Catherine A. MacKenzie –

Cathy escapes from her mundane world by writing poems and short fiction. Although she writes all genres, she often veers toward the dark and death, composing fiction most women can relate to. Although at first reading some of her stories might appear bizarre, they are so ominously real that one wonders what lives hidden within her mind. Cathy has been published in various print and online publications. She has also self-published several poetry and short story collections, available as e-books and print books on Amazon and Smashwords.

Cathy also paints, pastels being her favourite medium and her grandchildren her favourite subjects. She lives with her husband in Halifax, Nova Scotia. The couple winters in Ajijic, Mexico, where her works have appeared in local publications.

Visit Cathy's website at www.writingwicket.wordpress.com to discover more about this author and where to purchase her books.

Janet McGinity –

Janet was born in Moncton, New Brunswick to an Acadian mother and a father of Irish descent, and is fluently bilingual. She has been telling or writing stories all her life, and counts getting her first library card at age seven as among the most important events of her life. She was employed as a journalist with the Telegraph-Journal and Evening Times-Globe in Saint John, New Brunswick from 1982-1989, after obtaining a Bachelor of Journalism from the University of King's College in 1982. She also wrote short radio pieces and documentaries for CBC Radio in Moncton, and a few magazine articles.

Janet also holds a B.A. in Psychology (Waterloo), a diploma in Historical/Natural Interpretive Services (Seneca College of Applied Arts and Technology), a certificate in adult education (St. Francis Xavier) and studied folklore at Memorial University of Newfoundland.

She lives in Halifax, where after leaving journalism, she worked for the federal government, first as an interpretation specialist with Parks Canada, then as a Human Resources Advisor with a variety of federal departments. Now happily retired since 2009, she has time and freedom to devote to writing. She is currently working on a historical novel set in the 1870s in Jersey, Channel Islands, and Isle Madame, Cape Breton, along with shorter works of fiction. She is one of the founding members of Evergreen Writers Group.

Tom Robson –

Tom gave up writing creatively when the powers that be determined that untidy penmanship, erratic spelling, absent punctuation and grammatical inaccuracy were more worthy of their attention and criticism than his brilliant story ideas. But eventually he left school and, 20 years later found himself encouraging children to write, while satisfying his own urge to write with them and for them.

There have been many short stories and much personal writing. He likes to write poetry though it is not his forte. His one effort at a novel for middle grades won him first prize in the Atlantic Writing Competition in 1991. The necessity to revise and rewrite to satisfy publishers' demands was a writing requirement that frustrates him still.

There was a follow up success; second place in the Personal Writing category of the Atlantic Writing Competition for a story, "The First Time" or "All Those Days When the Earth Didn't Move."

His adaptation, into a performance piece, of "Peace Begins with You" by Katherine Scholes is published in Peaceful Schools and has been performed in many classrooms and as far away as Bosnia. Other original plays have been performed by his students in schools.

Currently, Tom writes for his own enjoyment and is collecting the many Scary Stories he has written for children, with a view to having them published. He also has a collection of personal reminiscences entitled "Long before Seventy Five," that he wishes to self-publish.

He thanks his spelling coach and very understanding wife and those long suffering students; the victims of his obsession. But they can write and he even thinks some enjoy doing so.

Arthur G. White –

In the dedicatory remarks of his book, Art writes: "To my Father, a letter-writing man, in whose likeness I'm proud to be compared." Also on that page was this: "To Henry Cowan, my boyhood English teacher, who valued a well-turned phrase above one purfectly spelt."

In the lee of those mentors, as a manuscript preacher, story-teller/writer, author and playwright, Mr. White has well-turned phrases all his life. His CV includes more than 200 magazine stories and articles in the United States and Canada, a collected work: "From Away, Here to Stay" and, in recent years, dozens of plays and historical readings, in which he has occupied roles as producer, director, actor, publicist and ticket-taker.

Says the author: "Thanks to Evergreen Writers for including 'Making it Happen' in their Anthology. It's a story I've been wanting to pass along for years...."

Wilma Stewart-White –

Wilma's fascination with the printed word started early in her life. A voracious reader and a journal keeper, the step into writing was natural. A business owner, museum curator, avid gardener and traveler, she lives in retirement in a very old house in Lunenburg County that holds its own secrets and ghosts. Her teacher training left her with a healthy respect for grammar and spelling and a deep and abiding love of books especially biographies and English novels. She is currently working on a mystery set in her small town.

Phil Yeats –

Phil Yeats lives with his wife of 40 years near the ocean in Halifax. He has a keen interest in environmental science and dabbled in yachting and golf before turning to creative writing. Phil is the author of two published short stories written using the pen name Alan Kemister, and is working on a mystery novel about a detective in a fictional town on Nova Scotia's South Shore. More information about these writing projects is available at alkemi47.blogspot.com.

***

The *Out of the Mist* Facebook Page:

https://www.facebook.com/EvergreenWritersGhostAnthology

***

www.ingramcontent.com/pod-product-compliance
Lightning Source LLC
Chambersburg PA
CBHW072132170626
46813CB00004BA/1535